Lock Down Publications and Ca$h
Presents

The Lane

Written by

Ken-Ken Sence

First Edition 2023

Printed in the United States of America

Lock Down Publications
P.O. Box 944
Stockbridge, GA 30281
www.lockdownpublications.com

Like our page on Facebook: Lock Down Publications
www.facebook.com/lockdownpublications.ldp

Stay Connected with Us!

Text **LOCKDOWN** to 22828 to stay up-to-date with new releases, sneak peaks, contests and more…

Like our page on Facebook:
Lock Down Publications

Join Lock Down Publications/The New Era Reading Group

Visit our website:
www.lockdownpublications.com

Follow us on Instagram:
Lock Down Publications

Email Us: We want to hear from you!

Dedication

First and foremost, I want to thank the Creator for blessing me with this opportunity. I would like to dedicate this book to three people: Carol Strick, a little Jewish lady who started all of this a long time ago. Never Challenge a taurus. If you read this or if anyone who knows her reads this, tell her to write to me. To the memory of one of my best friends: Christopher "Lil Chris" Pitts, it seems like it was yesterday and the pain won't go away. I miss you, my nigga. And to the memory of my other best friend: Brandon "B-Dub" McKeller, I miss you, bro. Me, you, and Chris— the streets should have been ours.

I also want to shout-out a few people: Robert "Lil Smurf" Alex, you are a true homie and I have nothing but love for you. Deuce-Deuce to the roof. To my nigga 4-4 (Fo-Fo), this is the result of all those late nights pecking on that typewriter while you were rocking out with Mrs. Harris. I told you I was going to do it. Next up, a bestseller.

I'm pouring my heart into every page, so if y'all like the book, write me and send me some feedback.

Send letters and feedback to:
Kendall Spence #1594392
Michael Unit 2664 FM 2054
Tennessee Colony, Texas 75886

Long Live The MANDINGOS

Prologue

Omar "Short Dogg" Wilson sat in his prison cell anxiously waiting for the day to be over. He was scheduled to be released the next day, and after five years of living in a small ass cell with another nigga, having lame-ass prison guards telling him what he could and couldn't do, and not being able to fuck a bad bitch when he wanted to, he was ready to get the fuck up out of that place and never return.

The only good thing about living in the cell with another nigga was the fact that he and his cellmate were from the same hood, and they repped the same set. They had known each other outside of prison before they had become inmates, so they respected each other's space and had a brotherly type of relationship. His celly was a few years younger than him, but WB3 was known throughout the streets of Dallas for being a nigga who would put in that work, and his murder game was official.

Short Dogg was an O.G. Everybody from Deuce Beckley knew him or knew of him, and if they didn't, they were false-claiming the set, and niggas got smoked for fuck shit like that. Short Dogg was a known beast in the streets. Niggas from the Triple D knew he was official. His cellmate was known as Brazy T, but most people just called him Brazy.

They were sitting in the cell smoking some Kush that an old-school boss lady, Short Dogg was fuckin', had brought him.

"Man, that shit J brought got me lit the fuck up," Short Dogg said, referring to Ms. Johnson who everybody called J.

"Me too, my nigga. I'm higher than a muthafucka. What you got planned after you touch down in the mornin'?"

"I'ma chill with the fam for a little while and I know my brothers got something planned for later that night. But after a few days of chillin' I'ma definitely get to the bag.

"What you gon' do about Yolanda? She still gon' be yo' number one?"

"Nah, my nigga. She good people and all but she ain't got what it take to hold a nigga like me down. When a nigga right there in her face and can touch her every night shit all good. But if a nigga gotta come do a little time she ain't made for ridin' a bid with a nigga. I'ma go through and fuck the shit outta her one last time, but I can't be in a relationship with her. She need a nine-to-five nigga and that ain't me, ya dig?"

"I feel you, big homie. She pretty, but being the kind of niggas we are, we gotta have that ride-or-die on our side 'cause ain't no tellin' when a nigga might have to come do a little time."

"That's it right there. I ain't no square ass nigga and that's what she need— a doctor or lawyer, or somethin'."

"What's up with them Glendale niggas? You think they still trippin'?"

"Blood, fuck them niggas. That's what it is we always trip with them niggas. They killed the big homie and then some of they niggas got popped in retaliation, so it is what it is."

"How them niggas catch the big homie Kool B slippin'?"

"The homie really played hisself over a no-good bitch. Big Blood was fuckin' with Kita. They had been fuckin' around on and off for like three years. She was throwin' a party so you know how them Oak Cliff parties get. Niggas from all hoods show up. Bloods wasn't beefin' with them niggas so nobody expected that shit to happen. We was all in the backyard dancin', smokin' and drinkin', and havin' a good time like niggas do. I think Kita went in the house for something and stayed gone a minute too long. When Kool B went looking for her, nigga found her in her room gettin' dicked down by that crip nigga, C-Money. Blood started trippin' and the nigga shot the homie like eight times. We heard the shots in the backyard but ain't nobody know what was goin' on 'til Kita came runnin' outside screamin' that the nigga had shot blood. We didn't find out 'til after the big homies from both hoods sat down and the truth came out.

"So they couldn't come to no kinda of peace treaty?" Brazy asked.

"They wasn't gon' hand that nigga over to us knowing a big homie had got smoked, and we wasn't gon' let that shit go down like that. We had to get at them niggas. The reputation of the whole hood stood on us gettin' back at them niggas, and they knew it too. They kept the nigga ducked off and guarded by five or six niggas every time he came outside, but he finally got caught slippin'.'"

"Hood Legend says you the one that done the nigga in— him *and* five of his homies."

"I can't confirm that," Short Dogg said, not looking for glory or fame.

"I feel you on that," Brazy said, not really expecting Short Dogg to answer the question.

Short Dogg thought back to that night…

He was fucking a bitch from the hood named Toya, who the nigga C-Money had been trying to get at too. Plus, they hustled on the block where she lived. Short Dogg hid out in her room until it got dark, and they came out on the block and started selling rocks and weed sacks off the porch of an old vacant house.

He was dressed in a blue North Carolina hoody, jeans, blue Chuck Taylors, and wore a blue bandana tied around his neck. He crept out of the back door of Toya's house and hid in the bushes watching. He stayed like that for hours listening to them talk and catch sells. He had an Uzi with a seventy-five-round clip inside it. He waited until he saw four of them, including C-Money, getting into a blue Caprice. He ran up on the car and let loose, spraying the car front to back. Then he turned the gun toward the other two who were still on the porch and let them have it too.

He ran back down the alley and hopped over two fences until he was on the side of the Camaro he'd borrowed from a dope fiend in the hood. He jumped in, started the car, and calmly drove off.

Once he got back to the hood, he pulled up to the big homie, Perk's house, where everybody hung out. He told him what he'd just done.

"Put that on the set," Perk challenged.

"That's on the set, O.G. I wet six of them niggas up."

"Hey, y'all grab the straps and three of y'all go to that end of the block and three of y'all go to the other end of the block," Perk said, pointing his index finger as he instructed the homies who had been hanging around outside. "Them Glendale niggas might be finna creep through," he alerted them.

They kept the block covered all night but the Glendale niggas never pulled up. That night the O.G., Perk, gave Short Dogg his O.G. status.

"What you thinkin' about, my nigga?" Brazy asked. "You had zoned out."

"In that world, my nigga. I'm ready to hit them streets."

"I already know it, my nigga."

"I'ma take a nap. Wake me up about nine thirty tonight so I can get ready for work. You already know J gon' wanna keep a nigga out there all night."

"I got you, Dogg. I'ma go to the dayroom for a minute and catch TMZ. I'll come wake you up 'bout nine thirty."

"Ah'ight."

Short Dogg lay down and drifted off into sleep and dreamed that he'd gotten out and become a millionaire. He was about to buy a Bentley off the showroom floor but just as the dream started to get good, Brazy woke him up.

He got up and took care of his hygiene and went out to work call, which was janitor duty— cleaning up the wing.

"Hey, baby," J said, as he walked up.

"What's up with it? I see you lookin' and smellin' good as always. Is there a special occasion?" he asked smiling.

"You know there is. We gon' fuck all night too. Mrs. Smith in the control picket so she gon' hold us down. Take some of those extra mattresses to the supply closet," she told him. "Let me go make my rounds and I'll be up there in a few."

"Ah'ight, I'm finna bang that back out," he said, staring at her wide, thick hips.

"You better," she said, laughing as she walked off.

Short Dogg stared at her ass as she walked away. She looked back over her shoulder, and when she caught him staring, she winked at him.

J was a bad bitch. She was in her early forties, honey complected, with big titties, and a fat, wide ass. She looked a lot like the actress Lisa Raye in the face. He really wanted to keep fucking with her but knew that wouldn't be a good idea right now. She wanted a man she could come home to every night. He knew she was a good woman, but he was too young and restless to settle down with just one woman in his life.

When she was done making her rounds, she went to the closet and found Short Dogg already naked and stretched out on the mattress.

"Omar, look at all that dick," she said, closing the door and taking him in her mouth. J was indeed a "head doctor". She gave him long, slow head until he sprayed her throat with his seed, and she swallowed it all.

"Damn, J, that shit was good."

"Now, I want you to fuck the shit outta me," she said, as she quickly unbuttoned her pants.

"Take them pants off. I'm finna suck that pussy first." Realizing that this might be the last time he'd see her, he was feeling some kind of way and wanted to do something special for her. He wanted her to know he really appreciated her and the things she'd done for him while he'd been locked up. Because of her, his time had gone by faster and it had been stress-free.

"Oh, shit, you gon' put that tongue on mama?" she asked playfully.

"Watch me," he answered, while simultaneously spreading her legs. She smelled like peaches. He licked and sucked on her pussy for twenty minutes causing her to have four back-to-back orgasms. She had cum so much, there was a puddle of cum underneath her when he finally lifted his head. He entered her wetness and pushed himself deep inside her and started fucking her.

"Oohh, Omar, I'ma miss this good ass dick. Take that condom off and fill this pussy with sweet nut." She reached down and snatched the condom off and put his dick right back inside of her. "Now beat this pussy up like you promised."

Short Dogg banged her back out for over an hour, and he didn't stop until it was time for her to go make her rounds and do her count.

They hurried out of the closet but not for long, because as soon as she was done they went right back in it and fucked until her shift was almost over.

"You got my number, so if you feel like you want to call me you know you can. I'ma miss you and I hope you stay safe and free," she told him, with tears in her eyes, before giving him a hug and a long kiss.

"I'ma miss you too, J. Thank you for helping me do this time and I'ma call you after I get settled."

"Take care, baby. Go on and get your stuff together. They'll be coming to get you around eight o'clock."

"Okay, J, be safe."

He went back to the cell and packed the little stuff he was taking with him, like his family pictures. He left the pictures of the homies and females from the hood with Brazy since Brazy had a thirty-year sentence for a murder conviction. He also gave Brazy his cell phone and weed.

"Well, fam, keep your head up and stay safe. Go check on my baby mama and my kids for me and send me a few pictures. I'll call you in a month or so after you get yourself together."

"Ah'ight, blood. I'ma go check on Tawanna and your kids and see why the fuck she ain't writin' you. I got you, my nigga, much love, homie," Short Dogg said, locking up with him and giving him a hug.

Short Dogg went to the administration building and signed his release papers before walking out of the front door. His baby brother Junior and his stepfather, who everyone called Pops, was waiting outside in a new Benz truck.

"What's up, big bro? You finally free," Junior said, giving him a hug.

"Hell yeah. What up Pops," he said, and leaned in to embrace him.

"Let's get the fuck outta this country ass town. This whole scene is depressing and scary as hell. All the years I was chunking rocks at this muthafucka and got away, to willingly drive up to this bitch is crazy."

"Bro, I got you some clothes in the back so you can get out that prison shit."

"Let me get that shit. I'ma change outta this shit right here and leave them they shit," Short Dogg said, grabbing the bag. He changed into some Robin's Jean, a red Polo hoody, and a pair of red Polo boots, then he balled up the prison

11

clothes and left them in the parking lot. "Let's get the fuck outta here."

Junior got in the back and let Omar get in the front. As soon as they were away from the prison, Junior fired up a fat ass blunt and handed him a bottle of Patrón.

"Welcome home, bro."

"Thank you, lil bro," Short Dogg said, and poured some Patrón in the paper cup Junior had given him. Pops, you want a cup of this shit?"

"And you know this, man," Pops answered.

By the time they got to Dallas, Short Dogg was asleep in the front seat. He'd been up all night in the supply closet lying next to J— due to the all-night sex mixed with the Patrón and the weed, he couldn't help but go straight to sleep. When he finally woke up, they were pulling up to his mother's house.

They got out and went inside. His mom, Faye, ran into his arms, kissing and hugging him all over.

"There go my baby!" she said.

"Mama, stop kissin' on me! You know what you and Pops be doing," he said laughing.

"Boy, shut yo' nasty ass up," Faye said, playfully punching him upside the head.

"Cock-blockin' young ass nigga," Pops said. They all busted out laughing.

He had already gotten his old school homegirl, Pat, to lease him an apartment in Bent Creek. Now, he was just waiting on the application to get approved so could get the keys. In the meantime, he stayed at his mom's house for three days and spent time with her.

He went to the strip club with his brothers, and they had given him a brick and ten racks to get back on his feet. He really didn't need the money because he had one hundred seventy thousand in his stash, but he took it anyway to keep from telling them all of his business. They even took him shopping and got him a whole new wardrobe. His oldest brother, Glenn, gave him a pound of dro and told him it was from Africa. The shit was so strong, it damn near gave him an asthma attack. Short Dogg had never seen any weed like that. It was white with purple spots in it. He tried to get Glenn to sell him a couple of pounds of the shit but he wasn't trying to hear any of that.

He got Junior to take him to his storage unit where he had his cars parked. He had a pearl-white Cadillac Deville Concourse and a candy-apple red Escalade on 28-inch rims. He very seldom drove the Escalade, except for when he wanted to stunt. He charged the battery up and drove straight to Jiffy Lube and had his oil changed and his tires checked. Then he went to the detail shop and got his shit washed and waxed. While they were cleaning his car, he walked over to the T-Mobile that was across the street to get the latest iPhone.

His truck was ready when he got back so he hopped in and left out of the parking lot of the detail shop, bumping "Trap Muzik" by T.I.

He drove down Forest Lane and got a room for two weeks at the Inn Town Suites, a small, discrete motel. He went to the store and got all the hygiene items he would need and a few boxes of baking soda. He then doubled back to the storage unit and got the brick his brother had given him and went back to the room. Once inside, he started cooking the powder up in the microwave.

He called his main niggas and told them to meet him at the room.

Lil Chris, B-Dub, D-Money, and Bobi were his arms and legs. They had grown up together in Oak Cliff. Plus, they had all hustled together before Short Dogg caught his time. They were all homies but Lil Chris and B-Dub were his main two niggas, just like Bobi and D-Money were tighter than frog pussy.

When they got to the room he laid the plot out to them. They had all been hustling together in Oak Cliff. The Oak

Cliff spot was doing numbers, but with four niggas in one spot and nobody on brick status yet, they weren't really eating like they wanted to. So, Lil Chris and B-Dub agreed to come to the North with Short Dogg and D-Money, and Bobi would continue to hold the D spot down in the Cliffs.

He fired up a couple of blunts of the African dro and damn near killed all four of them. The homies sat around kicking it and blowing smoke for a while. They were so high, one by one, they nodded off. They woke up a few hours later and headed back to Oak Cliff. They left Short Dogg to finish handling his business and gave him some time to get acclimated to being free again.

Not long after, he hopped in the shower, and when he was done, he got dressed in one of his new outfits. He pulled his dreads back and put a rubber band on them. Next, he threw on his Cartier frames and headed out to finally go do what he had been avoiding since he'd gotten home.

He pulled up at Yolonda's apartment and knocked on the door. She opened the door and smiled when she saw who it was. She wouldn't make eye contact with him so he thought she probably knew what was coming.

They hugged and kissed for a long minute. He couldn't help but stare at how beautiful she was. She was half Black, Korean, and Mexican. She was barely five feet tall but weighed about one hundred forty pounds, without an ounce of fat on her body— she was all ass, hips, thighs and tits. She was wearing a pair of boyshorts with a tank top and no bra.

"I see he's glad to finally see me again," she said, looking down at his dick print.

He didn't even try to respond. He just grabbed her little ass and ripped her tank top off and started licking and sucking all over her titties. He snatched her shorts off next, and the sight of her shaved, fat ass pussy sent him over the edge. He picked her up and pinned her against the wall with her legs on his shoulders and sucked her pussy standing up.

"Oh shit, Omar, suck my pussy good. Make me cum on your face baby."

He continued sucking on her clit while holding her in the air by her ass cheeks. He slipped the tip of his finger in her asshole and she instantly started squirting all over his face.

"Ahhhh, my pussy. What are you doing to my pussy, Omar?

I'm cummin' so hard... it won't stop!" she screamed, grabbing his head while humping his face.

"Let that shit out," he told her, still sucking on her clit.

"It's cummin', baby! It won't stop, I'm cummin' again. Oh shit, I missed you so much, so, so much! It's all over your face."

"I missed you too, mama. Damn, you taste like ice cream," he said in between lick's.

"Omar, I'm about to come again. Stick it in my booty again.

Make it squirt. Ohhh shit, it's squirting. I'm cummin', I'm cummin'."

"Let that shit go, baby. Let it all out," he told her, still licking her juices up.

After her orgasm subsided and she finally stopped squirting, he laid her on the hallway floor and ate her ass out.

"Oh shit, what are you doing to my ass?" she asked, trying to squirm away from his tongue.

"Don't run from it. Let me get my row out," he said in between her ass cheeks.

"Oh, my God! Why are you doing this to me? It feels so good, baby, eat this ass up!"

Somehow, he got his clothes off while still munching on her ass and slid into her pussy from the back. It felt like he'd stuck his dick into some hot water because her pussy was so hot.

"Damn, this pussy good," he told her, long-stroking her. Get on yo' knees, baby." He started banging her back out hard and fast.

"Oh shit, Omar, you fuckin' me so good."

After a while, he flipped her over and put her legs on his shoulders and slow-stroked her. They fucked like that for at least thirty minutes before he pulled out and nutted all over her stomach. He rolled off of her and they both fell asleep right there on the living room floor.

He woke up three hours later with Yolonda curled up next to him. She was lying on her side with her back toward him. He stared at her wide ass hips and felt himself starting to get hard again. He eased up behind her and slid right back inside of her.

"Oh shit," she said, waking up and looking over her shoulder at him.

"I can't get enough of this good ass pussy."

"Omar, I gotta tell you something. Oh shit, right there, hit it like that. Fuck, I'm 'bout to cum all over your dick."

When they finally made it to the bedroom, there were suitcases and clothes all over the bed. She quickly moved them and they got in the bed and continued to make love all night.

The next morning, they woke up and made love again in the shower. Then she cooked breakfast and they sat down to eat.

"Are you movin'?" he asked.

For a moment she became quiet and averted her gaze. Then she stared at him intensely as if searching for the right words. "I… um…I'm moving to Los Angeles. Sharonda asked me to move up there with her," she blurted without further delay.

Her sister Sharonda was in Los Angeles attending UCLA and had started modeling and doing commercials.

He didn't respond, so she said, "All you gotta do is tell me to stay and that we'll be married and live happily ever after," she said, looking at him.

"You wouldn't be happy. You know how I get down, how I get money. I'ma hustler and you need a nine-to-five nigga. That ain't me, Yolonda, and you know it. If sexual chemistry was all that a relationship was based on, we'd make a beautiful couple, but we'd both be miserable in life. Me, trying to be something I'm not, and you, being with a nigga who's not comin' home every night."

She was crying but she knew he was right. "I love you and I'll stay if you tell me to."

"I love you too but that's not enough to keep us happy. We gotta be compatible and you know we're not. I'd be selfish as fuck if I told you to stay. You're beautiful and sexy as fuck, but I want you to be truly happy. Go find you a nigga who will make you completely happy. I'ma hate to see you leave, but I know it's best for the both of us."

"I know you're right but I don't want to leave you."

"Come here," Short Dogg told her. She went and sat on his lap. "You just remember this *my* pussy," he said, pulling her shorts and panties to the side and rubbing her clit. I don't give a fuck who you with. When I come to Cali I'ma hit this pussy, ah'ight?"

"Oh shit …you got me so wet." She moaned.

He started rubbing her clit faster and stuck two fingers inside of her. "Tell me this my pussy."

"It's yours, it's yours… oh shit I'm cummin'!"

He pulled his fingers out of her pussy and stuck them in his mouth.

"You so nasty, boy," she said giggling.

"I know but yo' pussy taste so good," he said, pushing his plate away. He picked her up and sat her on the table and started eating her pussy as if it was dessert.

For two weeks, they stayed in her apartment making love— every day, all day, until the day came for her to leave.

He helped her load her luggage in her car and gave her twenty-five thousand out of the fifty thousand she had been holding for him. They had already discussed him taking over the lease on her apartment and moving in. She was also leaving him all of her furniture. They stood outside her car kissing for a long time before she finally got in the car and drove away.

He went back inside and smoked a blunt of the African dro and thought about how he had gone to prison. He had got pulled over by the law leaving this same apartment with a kilo of powder cocaine in the car. At the same time, he also thought about the fact that he was ready to get back to the money now that he was home.

He got dressed and left the apartment. He drove out of the parking lot bumping Big Tuck and rapped along with the music. "Dope boy clean not a damn stain on me...

Chapter 1

It was a hot summer day in July. The whole hood was out standing in the breezeway watching the drama unfold.

"Man, we gotta stop lettin' niggas come to our hood and murk our niggas," Big Mack said to the group of people, standing around watching the homicide detectives go in and out of the apartment where Lil Charles and his baby mama, White Tammy, had been found dead from gunshot wounds to the back of the heads. Their five-month-old son was found in his crib unharmed.

Lil Charles had been making a killing selling some of the best dro, Kush, popcorn, and X-pill's on the whole north side of Dallas. So, the hood knew he had been robbed and killed for his stash.

"Niggas act like we hoes or something out here, Big Mack continued. I'm from the Nawf, Nawf muthafuckin' Dallas and I'ma rep my shit. Today the last day for the bullshit. Lil Charles and White Tammy the last people from the hood a nigga gonna come over here and rob and kill. This the third time this year. Niggas know it's money out here to be made. This a million dollar lane and niggas preying on our hood. That's over! Either you niggas gonna rep and ride for Forest Lane or you niggas gone get the fuck off the block and stay off the block." Big Mack was one of the big homies in the hood, and to be just twenty years old, a lot of the young niggas looked up to him because they knew he was about that action.

There was over thirty people standing outside listening to what Big Mack was saying. It was official when Short Dogg spoke since he was a real O.G. and hood nigga. Especially since he had just come home from a prison bid and was already sitting on money,.

"That's law, Mack! You ain't even gotta keep goin' over what's already understood. You Lil niggas out hear robbin', stealin', fuckin' hoes, sellin' dope, and doin' grown-man shit, but niggas still keep runnin up in the hood and murkin' our people. They ain't doin' that shit down the street in Hamilton Park or down in Stoney Brook." Short Dogg was referring to the two hoods that bordered Forest Lane. In Hamilton Park they were Bloods, and in Stoney Brook better known as *Stoney Crook,* they were Crips.

"Today we startin' the M.O.B. If you ain't with it get the fuck off the block right now." Short Dogg paused for a second to let what he'd said sink in. They all knew what that M.O.B. stood for. "We 'bout to start murkin' er'thang that ain't from the hood. If you ain't ready to put in work for the hood then stay the fuck in the house and off the Lane." Short Dogg paused again looking around the crowd. "Now who down with the M.O.B.?" He stuck his hand out and Big Mack was the first one to dap in.

"I'm M.O.B.," Mack said.

"Me too," Lil Murda, Big Mack's ace said.

"M.O.B.," said Turk, Lil Chris, and Fred.

"M.O.B.," Rob spoke.

"Dub, what's up with you, nigga? You reppin' the hood or what?" Short Dogg asked one of his best friends who had been sitting back on the steps listening but hadn't dapped in yet.

"You already know I'm ridin' for the hood," Dub said.

"Nah, we don't know shit… that's why we dappin' in so we'll know what's what and who's what. Come dap in, my nigga," Short Dogg told him.

"Kim, what's up with you, Ericka, Kisha, and the rest of them lil fat butt ass girls over there? Y'all down with the hood or what?" Short Dogg asked, making all the lil hoodrat girls blush and laugh.

"We all M.O.B.," Kim said, staring her lil clique down to see if anybody wanted to buck her gangsta.

At about five foot nine, Kim was tall for a female. She was a cute Missy Elliot look alike, just a shade or two lighter. But she was thick just like Missy. Everybody in the hood respected Kim. She ran the biggest boosting clique in the north. Her girl's hit all the name brand stores and got only the top-of-the-line shit. Plus, Kim was known in the hood as a knockout artist so there wasn't a bitch in the hood who wanted to throw hands with her.

"Well, come on over here and dap in," Big Mack said to his big sister.

"Y'all listen, our hood runs from Skillman to Greenville on Forest Lane, and from Ashley Creek apartments to Church Hill Road on Audelia. Bent Creek apartments is our headquarters. We protect this spot at all costs. No outsiders hanging out and no drawing unnecessary heat to the HQ."

"Now, with that said, we gonna do this shit the right way.

Big Mack, Fred, Rob, Murda, Ronnie, and Kim, we all OGs but the rest of these lil niggas YGs and BGs. Y'all get ready to make some money 'cause we finna turn Forest Lane into the Carter," Short Dogg said.

Chapter 2

Short Dogg pulled up behind the warehouse a little after midnight. He was in a van from a carpet cleaning company that a female he had fucked a few times had let him use. For almost six months, he had been scoring a brick or two a week from a Mexican dude named Vinny. A few months prior, Short Dogg had bought two bricks from him that had been cut. When he dropped them in the pot to cook them up, he couldn't bring them back with the whip game. He ended up making very little profit off the work. Then when Short Dogg told him about it he acted like Short Dogg was the only person who had complained about the quality of the powder. So Short Dogg being a street nigga decided to take matters into his own hands.

For two weeks he followed Vinny. One night he followed Vinny to Flying J's Truck Stop where he saw him meet up and exchange duffle bags with a Mexican who was driving a black Expedition. Thinking he might be the plug, Short Dogg decided to follow the Mexican driving the Expedition.

Eventually, the Expedition led him to the warehouse he was now at. He had watched the building for a week and a half, day and night. He only saw two other people enter the building during those times, and each time they went in they carried a duffle bag, and each time they came out they carried a duffle bag. Short Dogg was convinced he'd found the stash house.

He watched the building for thirty minutes before he finally got out and made his way to the back of the building, where he had already peeped a window at the top of the building that stayed open.

He used the drainpipe and the side of the building to get enough grip to climb up to the where he could grab the ledge of the window and pull his body inside.

Once inside, he saw that he was on top of a shelf that was filled with lumber, plywood, and aluminum siding for houses. He paused for a long moment scoping the place out. When he felt comfortable that there weren't any dogs or surveillance cameras watching him, he climbed down and immediately started searching the building.

After leaving out of the garage area he walked down a hallway that had three closed doors. He opened the first room and saw five duffle bags just like the ones he'd seen Vinny and the guy in the Expedition with. He looked in the first bag and saw that it was filled with money. "Bingo," he said, looking in the other bags and discovering they were also filled with money. He dragged all five bags back to the window and dropped them outside.

He went back and went into the second room and found it stacked wall to wall with drugs. Cellophane wrapped bricks of cocaine, heroin, bags of methamphetamine, bags of ecstasy pills, and pounds of weed. He hurried to where he'd dropped the money and took it to the van. He emptied the duffle bags by pouring the money on the floor of the van then he ran back to the building and immediately started filling the emptied duffle bags with drugs.

When the five bags were filled, he went and dumped them in the van, then went back and repeated the process over and over until the entire room was vacant. By now, he was sweating like a runaway slave.

The third room was filled with enough weapons to start a war. He filled the duffle bag with automatic rifles and hand guns. He found several types of shotguns and took them too.

With his heart beating a mile a minute, he loaded over two hundred of the weapons in the van along with the money and drugs. He looked around one last time to see if there was anything he had missed. Satisfied with his haul, he finally climbed out of the window of the building for the last time and got in the van to leave.

He put his seatbelt on and started the van up and said a quick prayer before he drove off.

"Please, Big G, don't let the law pull me over with all this shit."

When he finally pulled up in front of the spot at Bent Creek he had tears in his eyes. He said another quick prayer and sat there for a moment just to let his heart rate and adrenaline return to normal.

He climbed to the back of the van and emptied the guns out of the duffle bags and put all the cash in the bags. He got out of the van and put the bags with the money in them in the trunk of his Cadillac Deville Concourse that he'd left parked in front of the spot before he went to hit the lick. Then he pulled out his cell phone and called Lil Chris.

"Say, You and Dub come out here to the parking lot and help me get this shit outta this van. Bring a couple of sheets," he said, before hanging up and waiting on them to make it outside.

When they made it to the van, Short Dogg opened the door. "Damn, Dogg, where you get all this shit?" Lil Chris asked, when they saw what was inside.

"Stop askin' all them rookie ass questions and help get this shit out the van and in the spot," Short Dogg answered.

They loaded the drugs in the sheets first and then carried them inside the house. Next, they got the guns out and took them inside.

Short Dogg counted the drugs with the help of Dub and Lil Chris. He had three hundred and twelve kilos of cocaine, three hundred pounds of weed, five million ecstasy pills, two hundred kilos of meth, and two hundred kilos of heroin.

"Blood where you come up on all this work?" Dub finally asked.

"I been had this shit put up. I had to move the shit with the quickness 'cause the lil spot where I had the shit got hot. Plus, the hood ganged up and on the set so I gotta put the niggas on."

"Blood, you rich," Chris said.

"Lil homie, I *been* rich, my nigga. I had all this shit before I got locked up. My nigga, I'm really a millionaire on the cool.

But dig this," Short Dogg said, twisting his niggas up in his game. You can't stunt on niggas who you fuck with if they broke and ain't tryna get no money. All that's gonna do is make niggas start hatin' and plottin' on you, tryna take yo' shit just 'cause they ain't got nothin', ya' dig?"

"I feel you," one of them said, while the other shook his head in agreement.

"But now the whole hood on the same shit we on. They mobbed up now, so we can't do nothin' but show the niggas some love. I told you niggas to get ready to make some money. We 'bout to get fed 'round this bitch."

"But y'all niggas peep this, and remember I told y'all this. Everybody ain't real and y'all niggas finna see how a little money will change a nigga." Short Dogg lit up a fat ass blunt of some purple and hit it a few times then passed it to Dub. "I feel you," Dub said.

"That's real shit, my nigga," Lil Chris chimed in.

"Never let this shit rule you," Short Dogg said, waving his hand toward the drugs and guns they had left on floor. "This shit comes and goes. If you smart with yo' shit you can keep havin' money. Don't let greed destroy no brotherhood or friendships. Money and bitches will tear down an empire if niggas let it."

***

25

Short Dogg spent the day getting the drugs and guns in a safe spot. After they counted the guns, they found they had over two hundred handguns, shotguns, and rifles, and just in case the law got on to him, or the jackboys tried to hit a lick on him, he played it smart and didn't leave everything in one spot.

As a precautionary measure, he took some of the drugs to the townhome of a White school teacher he was fucking with. He knew the laws would never suspect her and he knew he could trust her to the end. He took the guns and some of the drugs to a storage unit he'd rented, and it was also where he parked his tricked-out Escalade. He took the rest to a condo that only he and his brothers knew about; they only used it as a duck-off spot and to cook up work.

He returned the van to the chick who had let him use it and took an Uber back to his Caddy. Then he drove to Allen, a suburb outside of Dallas, where his mother and stepfather had built a half-million-dollar home. His mother was an only child and when her mother died, she'd left her an insurance policy. Since she was already a registered nurse working for other people, she used the money to buy the home and start her own home health care service.

He and his mother were more like sister and brother. They had a bond that was unbreakable, and they were as tight as a mother and son could be. On top of that, he and his stepfather were as tight as thieves. He had a brother and a sister from his mother. His sister Connie was a year older than him and seven years older than their baby brother Junior. Short Dogg and Connie had the same father, but he had died in a car accident when they were toddlers. His stepfather, who everyone called Pops, was Junior's biological father. Short Dogg loved the fuck out of his stepfather because he had been with his mother ever since Short Dogg was five years old. If truth be told, Pops was really the only father he'd ever known.

***

Short Dogg walked through the front door and went to the den. His mother and Pops sitting on the couch smoking on a blunt.

"What I done told yo' young hardheaded ass about just bustin' up in my shit without knockin' or ringin' the doorbell? One of these days I'ma end up poppin' yo' ass by accident 'cause you don't know how to knock, and it's gone hurt me to my heart. What if I was up in here gettin' some head from yo' daddy, and you just come bustin' up in here and fuck a bitch whole groove up," she said, teasing her oldest son. She was always happy to see him.

"Faye," Pops said, "stop playin' with that boy like that! You know I don't eat no damn pussy!"

"Stop lying!" Short Dogg and Junior said at the same time. Junior had walked in just as the words had left Pops' mouth

"Stay out my bidness, young ass niggas," Pops said, as they burst out in laughter.

"What you got goin' on that got you visitin' on a weekday?" Pops asked, while Short Dogg was shooting a couple of jabs and overhands at Junior.

He went over and kissed his mother and hugged Pops before he answered, "Let me holla at you and Junior for a minute," he said, before heading to the door and leading the way outside to his car. When they got to his car, he opened the trunk. "Yo, both of y'all grab two of those bags and take 'em to the entertainment room," he instructed them.

"What's in the bags?" Junior asked.

"You about to see if you go 'head and grab two of 'em and take 'em in the house like he asked and stop askin' questions. We out here in the driveway with all these nosey ass white people peekin' out they windows," Pops said.

"School that young nigga, Pops," Short Dogg said, poking his baby brother in the ribs, before grabbing a bag himself.

They went back inside with the five bags. When they bypassed his mother, she glanced at the bags but continued smoking her blunt and watching TV. She knew Pops was gonna lace her later on because that's just how tight they were. They didn't keep shit from each other, especially when it came to their kids.

The entertainment room was where the men in the family came to hang out, watch football games, boxing, or NBA games. A 72-inch flat screen hung on the wall. The room had a pool table, domino tables, Xbox, Play Station, a wraparound sofa, eating tables, and a fully stocked bar.

Short Dogg unzipped one of the bags and dumped its content on the pool table. Stacks and stacks of hundred-dollar bills covered the green felt of the table.

"Oh shit!" Junior said, grabbing one of the other bags and dumping it out on the table. His bag was filled with hundred-dollar bills, too. "Holy shit! Look at all this money! Pops open up yours."

"Gotdamn! It's the same thing in mine, too," Pops said, opening the bag wide and dumping the money on the table.

"I need y'all to help me count this," Short Dogg said. [1]

"Bro, these all hundreds, fifties, and twenties," Junior said, flipping through the stacks.

"Junior go get the weed box and some cigars from yo' mama and I'ma make us some drinks," Pops said. When Junior left the room Pops turned to Short Dogg. "Put me up on game, baby boy," he probed with a smirk.

Short Dogg ran the story down to him as Pops headed over to the bar, got three glasses, and poured Patrón in them. He told him about the drugs and the guns he'd stashed too. Just as he was finishing the story, Junior came back in the room with the weed box.

"Roll that shit up Junior," Pops told him. Then he turned and asked Short Dogg, "Who went on the lick with you?" Pops knew how niggas ran their mouths, so his first thought was if his son was in any danger of the Mexicans finding out who'd hit the lick and retaliating.

"You know me, Pops. I do my dirt by myself. I know I ain't gonna tell on *me*. The only other people who know anything is Dub and Lil Chris 'cause they helped me get the guns and drugs outta the van. But I twisted them niggas up into thinkin' I already had the shit stashed before I got locked up. They think I moved it 'cause the spot I had it at got hot. And they don't know shit about the money."

"Good, so we ain't gotta worry about nobody runnin' their mouth and bringin' no heat," Pops said, and at the same time handed Junior one of the glasses with Patrón. "Fire that smoke up and let's count this bread."

They spent the next six hours counting and arranging money in stacks of ten thousand. When they were finally done, they had three million nine hundred thousand dollars.

"Damn, I'm tired," Short Dogg said.

"Let me go holla at yo' mama. You know she wonderin' what we got goin' on since we been in here so long," Pops said.

"Bro, what you gon' do with all this money?" Junior asked.

"Bro, I'ma put on for the fam first. Then, after we all straight, we gonna show these niggas how to ball," Short Dogg said laughing. "But then, too, a nigga gotta be smart with this shit and do something legal to keep the money comin' in," he added.

"I called your brothers. They on their way out here," Pops came back in the room and told Short Dogg. He had three boys from an earlier marriage who were deep in the streets, getting money. "Let's run up here to the steakhouse and get something to eat while we wait on them to get here," he suggested.

Short Dogg pulled out his phone and called his sister. "Hey lil bro," she said, answering on the second ring.

"What's up? What you doin'?"

"Nothin', about to leave work," she said.

"You need to come out here to mama house."

"Why, is everything alright?" She asked in a concerned tone.

"Yeah, everything good, so calm yo' ass down."

"Boy, you scared me."

"Everybody on their way out here, so you need to hurry up."

"What's goin' on?"

"Is you comin' or not?"

"Yeah, I'm on my way," she assured him.

"Well, you'll find out when you get here," Short Dogg said before hanging up.

Junior and Short Dogg hopped in his Caddy and followed his mother and Pops to the steakhouse. While driving, Short Dogg called two of his closest homies who he'd met while in prison and had kept in touch with. He knew he was about to flood the streets and he needed manpower he could really trust because Dub and Chris wouldn't be enough to handle what he had in mind. First, he called Big Dre up in Austin, Texas.

"What's up, big boy?" he said, when Dre answered.

"Ain't shit. I just got off work and I'm tired as fuck. What you got goin' on down there in the Triple D?"

"I'm rich nigga, real talk. You ain't never gotta work again. Gas yo' shit up and come to the city tonight, nigga. I need you big time."

"Stop playin', nigga."

"Nah, real talk. I need you down here right now."

"You in some trouble?"

"Nah, nigga. I got a hundred stacks for you, so get yo' ass down here."

"Shit, I'm on my way. Give me four or five hours."

"I'm callin' George as soon as I hang up with you."

"You for real, ain't you? Nigga, what you done did?"

"I'll see you tonight. Call when you 'bout thirty minutes out," Short Dogg said, before ending the call. As soon as he had hung up, he called George down in South Dallas, another homie he'd met in prison.

"What up, lil nigga?" George said, answering the phone.

"I just got off the phone with Big Dre, and he on his way down here. When he get here, I'ma call you. I need you to meet us."

"What's up, nigga, you ah'ight?" George asked, always ready to put in work.

"I'm good. I'll holla at you tonight."

"Ah'ight, just hit me when Dre pull up."

They went inside and ate a quick meal. When they were done eating, they sat for a while and conversed over drinks until Pops said, "Let's get back to the house. The boys probably done made it by now."

When Junior and Short Dogg pulled up to the house, they saw his oldest brother's truck, so he knew his other brothers had ridden with him.

"How the hell y'all get in my house?" Faye asked, joking with the boy's.

"I got a key," Glen, the oldest boy said. He was thirty-four years old and had been in and out of the dope game since he was a teenager. His best friend had a Mexican connect who they got bricks from on the cheap.

"I don't need a key, I can pick a lock," the next to the oldest, Jay said.

"I hope you can pick some bullets out yo' ass too if you break in my shit 'cause I'ma damn sho' bust a cap in that ass," Faye said, looking like a thicker Angela Davis, with ass and hips for months.

"I'm packing right now," she said, showing them her license to carry a concealed weapon.

"Damn," they said in unison.

"Ma on some real live gangsta shit," Junior added.

"I been on gangsta shit, lil nigga. Don't let this nine to five shit fool you. Who you thank y'all got this gangsta shit from? I'm from Oak Cliff, Deuce Deuce Beckley," Faye said, twisting her fingers up and throwing up her hood. She turned and walked up the stairs. "Now, I'm 'bout to go take a shower," she mumbled to herself.

Everyone in the room stared at Faye, stunned and in silence, until Dell, the next to the youngest boy said, "Damn, ma real as fuck."

"That's why I been married to her for so long, and it gets better every day. I ain't never lettin' her go," Pops said, still in awe of the woman he'd married over twenty years prior. Now, let's go handle this business," he told his sons.

While Pops made more drinks for everybody, he told Short Dogg to run the play down to his brothers. Just as Short Dogg opened his mouth to speak, Connie walked in the room looking like a younger and thicker version of Faye.

She was dressed in a form-fitting Gucci dress that showed off her wide hips and voluptuous ass. When Short Dogg saw her he immediately thought, *she ain't got no business wearin' that up in no school tryna teach no lil boys*. Connie was a schoolteacher who taught fourth graders. If Faye had "ass for months" then Connie had "ass for years".

"Hey, y'all," she said, as she entered the room and gave everyone a hug.

Faye walked back in and hugged her daughter. She sat down so she could listen as Short Dogg ran the story down to them. He started at the beginning and told them how he'd hit the lick and filled them in on how much money and drugs he'd gotten out of the safehouse.

"Now we need to get this work off without the city knowing Omar hit the lick," Pops said, calling Short Dogg by his government. "Glenn what you think?"

"Look, Pops, Omar hit a nice lick, so I suggest we break this shit down to ounces, half bigs, and bigs. Maybe some quarter keys, but nothing bigger than that. Me, Jay, and Dell will cook some of the work up and cut some of the bricks down to snortin' powder. We gon' put the whip game down on it so we can flip it and get the most outta every brick"— Glenn paused a minute to think before he continued— "We gon' flood this bitch slow and methodically.

Omar, you got all them young niggas over there you fuck with, so get them niggas ready to hustle and let's put they ass to work. We need about six spots in different areas of the city. We gon' go to the townhouse and start cookin' the shit up tomorrow. Give us a week or so, but in the meantime you can start pushin' the weed, pills, and ice. I don't know shit about the heroin."

"I got my nigga, Big Dre, coming from Austin tonight to work his magic with that H. You know that's what he was locked up for," Short Dogg explained.

"Bro," Jay said, "you might wanna get more spots than that. I don't think you ought to sell more than one drug at any particular spot. Just speaking on some longevity shit."

"That's a good idea. You don't want too much traffic at one spot. Can you handle that, lil bro?" Glenn asked.

"I got that. I'ma get all my niggas together tomorrow and put them on point. Y'all handle that business and I'ma handle the other part," Short Dogg assured them. "A'ight, Pops, give them niggas two hundred a piece."

"Two hundred what?" Connie asked, still not understanding just how big of a lick Omar had hit.

"Two hundred thousand, Connie," Short Dogg answered.

"Ooh shit! You for real, Omar?"

Pops walked back in the room with one of the duffle bags and started counting out money on the pool table.

"Thank you, Omar," Connie said, giving him a kiss on the cheek.

"You know I got you, sis."

"Hey, don't nobody start ballin' outta control. Y'all be cautious how you spend this money. We don't wanna draw no heat on the fam," Pops said.

"Omar, you need to keep scorin' from that Mexican. You stop fuckin' with him all of a sudden and he gon' know you hit the lick, dig?" Dell said.

"Yeah, he right," Pops agreed, as he continued to count and pass out money.

"That's a good idea. I got you on that," Short Dogg said. "Pops you and mom get y'all five hundred thousand, give me four hundred thousand and put the other two million up for me," he added.

"Thank you, baby," Faye said.

"Let's get to work, y'all," Pops said, letting them know the meeting was over. "I got you, Omar, and 'preciate that, baby boy."

Chapter 3

"I'ma 'bout twenty minutes out. Where you at?" Big Dre asked when Short Dogg answered the phone.

"Meet me in the south at my brother's bar, *The Red Door*. You remember how to get there?"

"Yeah, I'll be there in a few."

Short Dogg hung up and immediately called George. "We on our way to *The Red Door*."

"I'm right down the street in the hood. I'll be there."

***

Omar "Short Dogg" Wilson was born and raised in Oak Cliff, his neighborhood was Deuce Deuce Beckley. When Short Dogg was in middle school they moved to the Ellum Thicket neighborhood of North Dallas when Pops inherited his home from his dad.

Short Dogg was a neighborhood Deuce Deuce Beckley Blood. The whole Ellum Thicket neighborhood was five Deuce crips. He was always going back to his old hood hanging out with his homies. After years of putting in work for the hood, he was promoted to O.G. status after one of the hood O.G.s was shot and killed at a house party, and he revenged the death. The whole hood knew who the murderer was, but nobody could touch him because he stayed surrounded by his crew, the Glendale Park Rolling Sixties Crips.

One night, Short Dogg dressed in all blue and went to their hood and saw the nigga sitting in a car surrounded by his crew. Short Dogg walked right up on them and unloaded an Uzi, killing all six of them.

Nobody in Short Dogg's hood knew what he was going to do until he got back and told the O.G.s what he had done. He was given O.G. status that night and given permission to start his own set in the north.

Six months later Short Dogg went to prison for a half brick of powder cocaine. He ended up doing four years on a five-year sentence before they let him out on parole. He had met Big Dre and George while locked up.

He had his twelve front teeth covered in 14 karat gold and red diamonds, and people knew he was on the red team when they saw him. When he hit the prison he moved in the cell with George, and Big Dre stayed in a cell up the stairs. The three of them became cool and vowed to stay in touch once they were released.

Big Dre was the first to get out and he stayed in touch until George got out. When Short Dogg finally got out, they threw him a welcome home party with strippers, champagne, and a lot of 'dro.

Short Dogg pulled up to the bar and went inside. He spotted George sitting in one of the back booths sipping on a drink.

"What the hell you done went and got yo'self into now?" George asked, before Short Dogg could even sit down.

"Everythang good," he answered, looking around to see if his brother was there.

"I can't wait to hear this shit," George said, shaking his head. "There go Big Dre comin' through the door right now."

Big Dre was about six foot five and weighed about three hundred and fifty pounds. He looked like Suge Knight with dreads. George was about six feet, light skinned, and looked like Dak Prescott.

"Come on, lil nigga. Sit on that side with George— a big nigga need a whole side," Dre said.

"Fat ass nigga," Short Dogg and George said at the same time.

"Now why you got a nigga way out here in the Triple D?" Dre asked. "This shit better be good 'cause I'ma miss work tomorrow and I'ma probably get fired," he concluded.

Before explaining why he'd summoned them, Short Dogg ordered Bud Lights and a shots of Patrón for everybody. Then, he went on to tell them about the lick he'd hit and about the drugs and money, however, he chose to leave out the amount of money and drugs he'd scored in total.

"How much money you hit for?" Dre asked.

"Fuck all that… just know I'm rich, bro. I need you to cut the heroin for me and help me get it off. You the only nigga I know who know how to fuck with the shit. My brothers don't even know how to fuck with it."

"I got you," Dre said nodding.

"What's up with you, George? You wanna get off some of this work?" Short Dogg asked.

"Bro, I'm all the way outta the game. I'll get some of my lil niggas in the hood to fuck with you and hook you up with them. How many you got and what's the price tag?" George asked.

George had gotten out of prison and married the vice president of a hospital. He'd met Kawanna through some friends while still on lock. She'd stayed down with him during his whole bid, and when he was finally released he married her. Short Dogg and Dre had been his best men at the wedding.

He wasn't about to get back in the game because he'd made a promise to her while he was locked up, that he wouldn't get back into that life once he got out. Plus, he didn't need the money since his wife was damn near rich and he still had some of his hustling-days money.

George was a neighborhood Blood reppin' Forty-Four Oakland in South Dallas. The whole south was a million-dollar spot when it came to selling drugs.

"Let's roll out. I got something for y'all out in the car." Short Dogg took them outside and gave each one of them a hundred stacks. Big Dre's eyes damn near popped out of his head.

"How much is this?" he asked.

"That's a hundred stacks, my nigga."

"Damn, I love you, fool," Big Dre said, grabbing him into a bear hug.

"Let me go, fat ass nigga, fo' you choke me to death."

"'Preciate this bag, lil nigga," George said, locking up with him. Call me when you ready," he added, getting in his car.

Chapter 4

Short Dogg took Big Dre to the duplex and told him to make himself comfortable. He owned the duplex, and it was where he, Lil Chris, and B-Dub lived. After dropping him off, he left to go handle his business with the M.O.B.

He went to the spot where he'd set up a meeting with all the O.G.s. Lil Chris and Dub were the only people present who weren't O.G.s. Once everyone had arrived, he lay down the plan.

"Look, I need all of y'all to get three spots and get some teams together. We need three to four people in each spot. Mack since you familiar with the Pleasant Grove area, you set up shop in the Grove. Rob, you know the west, so you set up shop in the west. Murda, all your people in the east so you set up shop over there. Ronnie, you set up shop in Oak Cliff, and Kim you stay out here in the north with me.

Kim, you put two niggas in each one of those spots with them girls. Don't have them in no spot by they self. Right now, we got weed, X pills, and ice, and the powder and hard will be here in a few days. I'm giving each one of y'all ten pounds of weed, a hundred thousand X pills, and a brick of ice. When I get the powder and hard, I'ma give y'all a brick of each. Plus, I'ma give y'all a brick of heroin. Break the shit down and get some money. We ain't sellin' no weight right now, we strictly gettin' the bag. Dub, you and Chris roll up some blunts of that shit we 'bout to flood the city with and bring that Patrón and some cups in here," Short Dogg told his lil niggas before he continued.

"I need fifty stacks back from each one of y'all. That ain't shit since y'all gonna make a mil off the X pills alone. Make sure y'all teams paid right. We all fam and we ain't crumbin' nobody who down with the M.O.B."

They poured up and fired up as they continued to make plans and get all the details ironed out. Just as the meeting was about to end, there was a loud commotion outside the spot and everybody grabbed their strap and rushed outside.

This M.O.B. nigga name Kels was squaring up to go hand-to-hand with a nigga known as Big Jim, and there were about ten or fifteen M.O.B. niggas and bitches standing around watching. Big Jim hustled out of the apartments and stood about six one and weighed about two hundred and twenty-five pounds. Kels was five feet eleven inches tall and weighed one hundred sixty-five pounds.

"This ain't what you want, lil Kels. I'm tellin' you, my nigga … I'ma sleep you, lil homie," Big Jim said, posting up.

"That's what you gotta do 'cause I'm damn sho' finna try and sleep you, my nigga," Kels said, living by the rules of the streets— strike first. He threw a four-piece combination at Big Jim.

Big Jim caged up and blocked most of the punches, then he shot a left and a right that Kels easily weaved. Being the smaller fighter, Kels was quicker and faster, but Big Jim was stronger and more powerful.

Short Dogg thought to himself… *if Kels stay on his toes and keep his endurance, he can win.* Just as the thought left his mind, Kels unleashed a flurry of rights and lefts, catching Big Jim square on the chin with several of them, before sitting him on his back pockets. He sat on the ground for a few seconds and smiled up at Kels, who was still bouncing around ready to go.

"Now, I'm finna beat yo' ass," Big Jim said. He got up and started stalking Kels. He knew he couldn't beat Kels boxing so he had to land some power blows to slow him down. He finally caught Kels with a wild overhand left to the temple that rocked him. He didn't go down, but after that punch Kels was out of it and Jim started catching him with some damaging blows, so Short Dogg stepped in and stopped it.

"It's over with, Big Jim," Short Dogg said, while stepping between them.

"Nah, my nigga, watch out," Big Jim said, trying to go around Short Dogg, "this what the nigga wanted so I'ma mash the nigga all the way out."

"That's not gon' happen," Short Dogg informed him. "I said it's over with so go on where you came from and be thankful you walkin' away."

"Man, you niggas got me fucked up! Y'all been runnin' around here like y'all own the whole block and I'm tired of this bullshit! Anybody else wanna step up, they can get the same thang Kels got."

"A'ight, Jim, you just let your mouth overload your ass. Now I wanna fight," Short Dogg said, simultaneously taking off his shirt.

"It's whatever on mine. I'ma sleep all you niggas out here today!" Jim said.

"I'm next then," Big Mack said. Now he was getting crunk.

"Chill Mack," Short Dogg told him. "I'm the last nigga you gon' ever wanna fuck with over here. I promise you that," Short Dogg told Big Jim. He had already peeped his boxing game and he could tell it was weak, and relied on his size and strength alone, but had no skills. As soon as they posted up, Short Dogg caught Jim with a straight jab to the chin.

"That punch was weak! Nigga, I eat shit like that all day."

"You ain't gonna keep eatin' them," Short Dogg vowed. True to his word, he fed him two more.

Big Jim tried to stalk Short Dogg like he'd done Kels, but Short Dogg had learned his fighting skills in the Texas prison system where all they did was fight for recreation. Big Jim charged him, but instead of dodging him, Short Dogg met the charge and dropped his head in Jim's chest and threw two overhand haymakers that landed on Big Jim's chin, instantly dropping him to the dust— he got knocked the fuck out.

The whole M.O.B. started clowning Big Jim. Kels ran over and kicked the shit out of him and one of the girls started doing the Tootsie Roll on top of the nigga. Short Dogg sat on the steps and smoked a blunt while he waited on Big Jim to wake up.

When Big Jim regained consciousness, Short Dogg passed the blunt to Lil Chris, looked at Big Jim and said, "Come on, my nigga, let's finish this shit·."

"I'm good, my nigga. You got that," Big Jim said, trying to tap out.

"I know you ain't tryna quit after all that big boy shit you was talkin' a few minutes ago. The same way you wanted to mash my nigga out, I'ma mash you out. You gon' respect this M.O.B. shit, my nigga," Short Dogg said. He hit Big Jim with a barrage of hooks that put him back on the ground, knocked out again.

"Roll me another blunt," Short Dogg told Ericka.

This time, when Big Jim woke up and saw Short Dogg waiting, he jumped up and took off running. A few M.O.B. niggas took off after him but Short Dogg called them back.

"Let the nigga go. The next time you see him tell him the M.O.B. said he can't live over here no more. He got seventy-two hours to get his shit and move. If anybody see him after that seventy-two-hour deadline, murk him."

"Y'all get busy and handle that business. Come through later on tonight and Dub and Chris will have those packages for y'all. Kim, call me later on I need to holla at you. I'm 'bout to go handle some business," Short Dogg said, getting in his car to go get Big Dre to handle the heroin.

Chapter 5

It was New Year's Eve and the whole hood was at the Bent Creek Apartments. The M.O.B. was throwing a New Year party and a coming home party for Big Mack who had just spent this last week in jail on a murder charge. A week prior, a Jackboy named Bud was hanging around the apartment complex. Big Mack told the fool to move around, but Bud who everybody in the hood knew, wanted to act tough.

"Say, bro, I already told you to get the fuck outta the apartments. Ain't no more hangin' out around the spot. Plus, you a fuck-nigga, lookin' to rob somebody. That shit dead over here, and if I find out you had anything to do with my nigga lil Charles and White Tammy gettin' killed, I'ma murk you. On gang, my nigga," Big Mack promised.

There were a few people hanging around outside, smoking and chilling. When Bud realized they were listening to he and Big Mack's confrontation, he tried to stunt, knowing he wasn't built like that. He knew he was fucking with a real live goon in Big Mack.

Bud had shot a few niggas, but he'd either shot them in the back or with a gang of niggas by his side who had his back.

"Fuck you, nigga! Ain't no nigga puttin' no limitations on where the fuck I can and can't go," he said, as if he was really about that life.

Big Mack knew Bud was an undercover bitch hiding behind his homies. With a quickness, he two-pieced him and dropped him to the ground before he started stomping the fuck out of the nigga.

"Nigga, this the M.O.B.! Recognize what the fuck goin' on around this bitch and don't come back over here, fuck boy."

Bud jumped up and took off running. "I'll be back. Y'all niggas wanna rat-pack a nigga," he shouted, without looking back.

"Listen to this bitch nigga. He know damn well ain't nobody touched him but me," Big Mack said to the people standing around watching. "That's what's gon' happen to any nigga who come around here without a reason to be here. Ain't no more hangin' around, it's sco' and go. Troy, you and Nate go sit in the front and let me know if that nigga come back. Call my phone as soon as you see the nigga," Big Mack said, lighting up a blunt, as he made his way back inside the spot.

About thirty minutes later, Troy called Big Mack. "Bro, that nigga went and got his brother Juwan. They just came through the front gate. They headed toward the back right now and that nigga Juwan got a gun in his hand."

"Ah'ight," Big Mack said. He grabbed his 9mm and stepped outside the front door. As soon as he stepped outside, he saw Juwan and Bud. He could see the gun in Juwan's hand and immediately started unloading on him, hitting him five times in the chest and neck.

Bud saw his brother fall and took off running for the second time in one day. Big Mack cocked his Glock without hesitation and busted it at him. The bullets hit him in the back two times but Bud never stopped running.

Big Mack ran up on Juwan and spit on him then kicked him. "This the M.O.B., ho nigga. Don't ever come over here with that ho shit. Now look at you, layin' in the dirt wet the fuck up. Yous a bitch boy," he said, and kicked the nigga again. "Somebody call the meat wagon for this bitch nigga. Let this be a lesson for all bitch niggas. This how it's goin' down on the Lane. Ain't no nigga comin' over here disrespectin'. We reppin' for the hood, hard," Big Mack said. After murkin' Juwan he was crunk.

When the police came they arrested Big Mack even though Juwan still had his gun in his hand.

"What up?" Short Dogg spoke, after answering his phone.

"Blood, Big Mack just murked that nigga Juwan. Twelve took Mack in even though the nigga Juwan had a pistol in his hand when he got wet up."

"Chill, not on the horn. I'm on my way to the spot."

"Twelve all over this bitch right now. I'll hit you when them hoes leave."

"Cool," Short Dogg said and ended the call.

He hired a lawyer for the case and it took a week for the lawyer to get the murder charge dropped to justifiable homicide. Big Mack was free and ready to bring in the new year.

***

Short Dogg pulled up to the Bent Creek apartments at 11 p.m. on the dot. He was rolling in his tricked-out, candy-apple red Escalade, sitting on 28-inch rims with the butterfly doors. It was fully loaded with a fifteen-inch TV screen, PlayStation, Xbox, 2 five-thousand-watt amps, and a Bose system that was banging so hard, it set off car alarms in the parking lot.

He was dripped out in a red Sean John outfit and a red Polo Bomber jacket, and Prada frames covered his eyes. He sported a fifty-thousand-dollar Rolex, and his necklace was a seventy-five-thousand-dollar, custom-made, diamond-studded chain and pendant that spelled out M.O.B. in red diamonds. It had been seven months since he'd hit the lick and money was pouring in. The whole set was getting money.

Big Dre pulled up right behind him and they stood out in the parking lot conversing.

"My nigga, you on yo' way to the federal penitentiary," Big Dre said, as he stood next to his new Dodge Ram truck.

"Why you say some bullshit like that, nigga?" Short Dogg asked suspiciously. He looked around to see if he could spot any undercover agents.

"How much you pay a month for these broke down ass apartments?" Big Dre asked, nodding toward the raggedy apartments.

"About six-fifty a month for a one bedroom."

"You payin' six-fifty a month? Now, look at all these hundred-thousand-dollar cars out here in a six-fifty a month parking lot," Big Dre said, gazing at Short Dogg like he'd already been indicted.

Short Dogg looked around and saw two Range Rovers, six Benzes, four BMWs, and several old schools that had been refurbished, candy painted, and sitting on huge, shiny chrome rims.

"Damn, you sho' right." Short Dogg had to admit the parking lot looked like a car show but nobody had a job.

"I'm not about to hang out over here with these young, dumb ass kids, and you better stop hangin' around here so much before you be lookin' at a conspiracy charge," Big Dre said, putting his homie up on game before walking away and heading back to his truck. "I'll fuck with you later this week at the Red Door. I ain't comin' back over here," he made clear.

Short Dogg went inside the spot and dapped everybody up. The whole M.O.B. was dancing, the blunts were going around, and the drinks were flowing steady.

"There go my muthafuckin' nigga, Short Dogg," Big Mack yelled over the music, and grabbed him in a bear hug. The DJ played Lil Boosie's "Wipe Me Down", and all of the

M.O.B. members stood around Short Dogg while pulling out stacks of money and wiping the big homie down.

Not long after, the dro', Kush, and drinks had Short Dogg feeling right. He was sweating like a nigga on his way to the electric chair. When he took his shirt off, all the little hoodrat bitches were jocking his muscular, tatted up body.

He was grinding on a short, thick, red bone, M.O.B. chick named Cassie, when big booty Shalika walked up and said, "Damn, bitch, you gon' hog the nigga all night?"

"Excuse me! I didn't know there was a line," Cassie said, with an attitude, before stomping off.

"Shalika, how you gon' just come fuck off the pussy I had lined up for later on?" he asked, throwing game at Shalika since he had no intention of fucking off any of his dick with Cassie.

"You can do way better than that. Plus, the whole M.O.B. done had that bitch. But, if you really tryna fuck off some of that dick, I don't have shit to do and I don't have to work tomorrow."

All the niggas on the Lane considered Shalika the baddest bitch to ever walk the block. Every nigga on the Lane wanted to fuck her but she had been fucking with some square nigga named Dinky ever since junior high school. He'd gone off to the military and she'd gone off to college.

She graduated from college and had been back in the hood for about a year. Shalika was M.O.B. but she worked every day and didn't take part in the criminal activities. Lil Murda had been trying to get at her since she had been back but she wasn't feeling him like that.

"So, what's up with that dick?" she asked.

"Shalika, if I give you some of this good ass dick I'ma fuck your whole life up," Short Dogg told her seriously, while grabbing his dick. "Plus, my lil nigga, Murda, gon' be mad at you."

"Boy, please! That lil dirty dick ass nigga, That nigga done fucked every lil hoodrat bitch around here. You know I ain't that kind of bitch. He'll never get this," she said.

"I don't just go around giving my dick away, so when I do I puts in that work."

"I'ma big girl, Short Dogg. I can handle my business without runnin' my mouth or gettin' in my feelin's."

"Nah, Shalika, you a real bad bitch, but I'm tellin' you, I got some good dick and I don't want this to come between our friendship. You heard what happened to your homegirl Trina, didn't you?" Short Dogg was talking about another bad bitch he had been fucking with from the hood, and she went to the crazy house after he'd cut her off.

"I heard about Tee. But she was a weak bitch anyway. I can handle it. I promise I won't start trippin'. Just let me get that dick tonight."

Shalika knew she was a bad bitch, and every nigga she had ever fucked had fallen in love with her. She'd only had three lovers in her whole life. Dinky, who she thought she was going to marry, had been stationed in Germany while in the army. Unfortunately for Shalika, he met a White woman who he fell in love with and married. After that, he decided he wasn't coming back to America.

She had always liked Short Dogg. His swag was right, and even though he was a pretty boy, he was all gangsta. There was no backup or backdown in him and that made her pussy wet, and her heart felt some kinda way. She figured if she gave Short Dogg the pussy he would get sprung. She was the kind of bitch who needed a good man to wake up to every morning, and she had her sights set on Short Dogg.

"Ah'ight, Shalika, I'ma bless you. But if you start trippin' and actin' crazy, I'ma act like I don't even know you."

"What if *you* start trippin'?" she asked smiling.

"That ain't gon' happen unless I want it to happen, and besides, I'm not lookin' for a relationship right now.

Anyway, you and me both know when Dinky come back from Iraq or wherever he at, you goin' right back to him."

"That's over. He in Germany and done married a White girl over there, so he ain't comin' back."

"Damn, that's fucked up," Short Dogg replied.

They stayed at the party until after midnight to bring in the New Year with the M.O.B. They popped the Champagne and drank a couple of bottles. Afterwards, Short Dogg and Shalika left in his truck and drove to the Palms apartments, which was where Shalika lived.

When they got inside, he noticed that she had a nicely decorated home. He walked around admiring the pictures on the shelves and Shalika stepped away to take a shower. While he waited, he smoked a blunt and watched SportsCenter.

Shalika was what hood niggas all across America referred to as a Stallion or Amazon. She was five foot eleven and kind of reminded you of a super-thick version of actress Meagan Good. She had a job, so she was making her own money, she had her own home, and her brand-new Malibu was sitting out in the parking lot. Surprisingly, she didn't have any kids and she was pretty. *If she don't start trippin' after tonight, I might fuck with her*, Short Dogg thought.

When she came out of the bathroom, she was wearing a red negligée. He had to admit, she was even finer than he'd realized. He recognized that she was going out of her way to impress him. He wondered what her angle was. He knew she didn't need him for his money. The thought that she might have had a crush on him, and had been liking him for years, had never crossed his mind. Short Dogg excused himself and went and got in the shower while Shalika rolled up more blunts.

He heard the first gunshots just as he stepped out of the shower and began to dry himself off. Immediately after the first shot sounded, he heard a succession of fifty to sixty gunshots, seemingly from several types of guns.

Chapter 6

Naked, and with his pistol in one hand and his phone in the other, Short Dogg exited the bathroom. He knew the shots were coming from the Bent Creek apartments. Shalika was already at the window looking out when he returned to the living room.

"What's goin' on over there?" he asked, walking up to the window.

"All I can see is a red truck turned over right outside the exit gate and a bunch of people runnin' or drivin' off."

Short Dogg looked out the window, and when he saw the red truck he didn't recognize it, so he called Lil Chris.

"What's up over there?"

"Big Mack and Lil Murda got into it with some niggas from the party and the niggas left and came back shootin'. The whole M.O.B. was waiting on them dumb niggas and wet they shit up. The truck flipped over right outside the back gate," Chris told him.

"Yeah, I see the truck," Short Dogg said.

"Damn, blood, you still over there? Bro, you gotta get the fuck outta there 'cause the laws finna shut that bitch down.

"Nah, I'm good. I'm in the Palms at Shalika spot."

"Ah'ight, I'll catch up with you tomorrow. Me and Dub headin' to the crib."

"Hey, who them niggas was?"

"Some nigga they call Bear outta East Dallas, and two more niggas."

"Ah'ight, I'll get at you tomorrow," Short Dogg said, and ended the call. He told Shalika what went down while still looking out the window.

"Damn, Short Dogg you got a big ass dick," Shalika said, staring at him with lust in her eyes, while reaching out caressing his dick. She dropped down to her knees and licked the head a few times.

"What you gon' do with it?"

"I'm finna eat this dick up," she said, with lust lacing her tone.

"Quit talkin' about it and be about it," Short Dogg said, grabbing the back of her head and guiding it to his dick.

Shalika went right in on his dick, licking and sucking on the head a few times before she swallowed all eight and a half inches. She held it down her throat and allowed her throat muscles to message his dick.

Damn, he thought to himself, *Shalika got some fire ass head.* But being the vet he was he started thinking about how he was gonna decorate the sports bar he was planning on opening.

After about twenty minutes of some the best head he'd ever had in his life, he couldn't hold out any longer. "Damn, I'm 'bout to nut.

"Mmm, I'ma swallow all that shit too," Shalika said, before swallowing his seed and milking him dry. She kept sucking him until she got him back hard, then she looked him straight in the eyes and said, "Get up in this pussy."

He got a condom out of his pants pocket and hit Shalika with that front, back, and side-to-side. For three hours, he punished her pussy in every position he could think of.

He started on the couch with her on her knees so he could watch that big ass jiggling while he slammed dick to her. Then he moved her to the bed where he slow-grinded her pussy for a long time.

"Oh my God! This the best dick I ever had in my life! I'm cummin' again. Oh shit... no, no, no, take it out. I can't take no more, Short Dogg," she said, not really wanting him to take it out. He had been putting it on her so good, she was confused about the sensations she was feeling in her pussy.

Short Dogg laid on her with the dick in her for about five or ten minutes without moving. Then without warning, he lifted her legs up and commenced to banging her back out.

"Baby, I love you, Short Dogg. This your pussy forever. Oh shit, I'm 'bout to nut again. This the tenth nut. Oh shit, I'm nuttin' again… Oh my God, oh my God! Yo' dick game is bananas."

Short Dogg fucked her until she passed out and started snoring like an old woman. As she lay sleeping, he got up and rolled a blunt and hit the Patrón before he joined her in sleep.

A few hours later, Short Dogg was awaken by someone knocking on Shalika's door. He looked over at her and saw that she was in a deep slumber. He shook her awake— "Somebody knockin' on your door."

She got herself together and got up to answer the door. After a few minutes, Short Dogg heard Lil Murda's voice. He could tell he was drunk because his words were slurred and he was talking way too loud. He got up and put his pants on.

"I seen you all on the nigga Short Dogg dick last night. What? You done turned into the rest of these bitches chasin' a sack?" Lil Murda said.

"What the fuck you all in my business for, nigga? I ain't got no man," Shalika responded, clearly aggravated.

I already told you that I want that pussy and Short Dogg or no other nigga gonna come between what I'm feelin' for you. So you might as well get that through your head. Short Dogg don't want you he just tryna fuck."

By now, Short Dogg had heard his name too many times so he stepped in the room and addressed the situation. "You doin' a whole bunch of hatin' and talkin' down right now, blood, when you really ain't got no business with my name in your mouth."

"Nah, nigga, I don't talk down on no nigga."

"Blood, you might wanna go sleep that liquor off 'cause right now that shit got you feelin' like Superman and you 'bout to get yourself in a jam."

"Can't no nigga *jam* me, nigga. *I jam* niggas."

"Come on outside to the parkin' lot since you talkin' that big dog shit. I'ma show you this paddle."

"You got me fucked up. You ain't said shit," Lil Murda said and headed for the door.

As soon as they got outside, Short Dogg noticed Big Mack sitting in the passenger seat of Murda's Range Rover. He saw them head to the parking lot so he hopped out of the truck.

"What's up, blood?" Big Mack asked Short Dogg.

"I'm finna spank this nigga ass."

"Nah, Dogg, I can't let you get at my nigga like that," Big Mack said.

As soon as the words left his mouth, Short Dogg turned and hit him with a four-piece combination. He put all his power in that last punch which was a right hook to the chin, that caused Big Mack to crumble to the ground, sleep.

Short Dogg never stopped moving. Just as Lil Murda was putting his fist up, Short Dogg caught him with a right and a left. Lil Murda took the two piece and threw a right and a left back at Short Dogg which he blocked with his shoulders and forearms. Short Dogg countered with a short right to the chin, a left hook to the temple, and a right uppercut to the chin that dropped Lil Murda to the asphalt, knocked the fuck out.

***

Short Dogg helped Big Mack up and walked him over to the truck. He talked to him about what had just happened between them.

"Damn, Dogg, I'm sorry shit had to go down like this but yo' boy was way outta line. Call me in the mornin' and I'ma run it all down to you," he told Big Mack.

He went over and helped Lil Murda up and helped him to the truck. "Blood, I been too good to you for you to let a ho come between family. Call me when you sober up and we'll talk." When Short Dogg got back up the stairs, he immediately started getting undressed.

"You better watch Lil Murda and know he'll never forget that," Shalika told him.

He didn't even respond. He was still wired up and his adrenaline was pumping. He planned on taking it out on Shalika's pussy. He pulled out a condom and started putting it on.

"What's up, Short Dogg?" she asked, looking Paranoid.

"I'm 'bout to get back in that pussy before I go."

"Short Dogg, I can't take no more dick right now. You fucked the shit outta me last night and my pussy sore."

"I thought you was 'bout that life … all that big girl shit you was talkin' last night. Don't tap out on me now. I thought you was a soldier?" he asked, pulling her to the edge of the bed.

He slid inside her wet pussy and started slow-stroking her.

"Oh shit! Oh shit, that dick good," Shalika screamed, rolling her hips and throwing the pussy back. "Damn, I'm 'bout to nut all over that dick. Beat it up! Oh shit, I'm nuttin'!"

Short Dogg let her calm down after she nutted, then he started banging her pussy like it was a set of drums.

"Oh shit, Short Dogg! You hurting my pussy, but it feels so good. Don't stop! I'm finna cum again. Oh shit, you a beast. Fuck this pussy!" Shalika cried, getting into it, throwing the pussy back. "Kill this pussy, baby! Murder that shit! It's yours! I ain't gon' never give your pussy to nobody else. I'm cummin'…"

Chapter 7

2005 was a catastrophe for the people of New Orleans and Mississippi, but a hustler's heaven for the hustlers in Texas. Hurricane Katrina brought millions and millions of dollars to the illegal drug trade in Dallas. When the evacuees got settled in and the FEMA money started coming, Short Dogg was making over a hundred thousand a day.

He had found a connect on the X pills through Big Dre. Dre hooked him up with a Vietnamese that was selling him the pills at twenty five cent a pill when he got a hundred thousand or more. He was killing the game with the pills. He would sell them for two dollars a pill whenever the customer bought a hundred or more. He still had bricks of ice that he was breaking down and selling by the ounce.

His brothers had worked their magic with the powder. They turned a hundred bricks into two hundred by cutting it with Superior B. They only sold it as snorting powder. Every brick they cooked up was stretched to fifty ounces.

Big Dre did his best shit with the heroin by dividing one brick into bricks of three. He started calling his old customers and shit was selling like hot cakes.

Short Dogg had already put the hood on. He was done giving out free dope. Everybody was on their own as far as keeping their individual spots rolling. If they wanted more dope they had to pay for it. He had four spots that were rolling off the chain. He had opened three sports bars that he'd gone half on with Lil Chris and B-Dub, and a club that he'd gone half on with his little brother, Junior. The money was coming in fast and he was showing Dub and Chris how to make legal money instead of staying in the trap all day.

***

They were in the back of Bent Creek outside the spot Chilling. Short Dogg, Big Mack, and Lil Murda was back on speaking terms. However, he could tell that Lil Murda was still in his feelings about taking that "L".

"Blood, the Lane getting hot as hell," Lil Chris said, as he watched a police car roll through the apartments. "The laws stay rollin' through this bitch.

"Yeah, 'cause Big Mack and Lil Murda stay on some dumb shit. Then they go back to their spots after makin' it hot over here," Dub added.

"Them niggas can't be makin' no money 'cause they stay over here too much," Chris said. "Plus, Big Mack got two or three pistol cases pending. All his money going to lawyers and the bail bondsmen."

Short Dogg was just chilling, smoking a blunt, and listening to his lil homies vent. But he knew what they were saying was true.

"Y'all niggas better be savin' y'all money up 'cause I'm 'bout to get all the way out the game and get this legal money." It was the first time he'd spoken to his niggas about what he was planning. "Dub you and Chris should have over a million in the stash 'cause y'all ain't been fuckin' off no money. "Chris," Short Dogg said, turning toward him, "at twenty three, you got three kids already, nigga. So you really need to be puttin' your money up. And you need to get Tawanna a house and out that apartment so your kids can have a real home."

"Yeah, I been thinkin' about that," Chris admitted.

Just as they were getting deeper into the conversation, they suddenly heard gun shots coming from the front of the apartments. They ran out to the parking lot where they could see the front of the apartments and saw a light skinned nigga, with a pistol in his hand, get into a gold Cadillac and peel off.

"That was ole' boy who fuck with that New Orleans bitch up front on the third floor," Chris said.

"Dub, get the choppa and let's see what's poppin'," Short Dogg said.

Before they could get to the front, a nigga named Tip came running to the back screaming, "That nigga just murked Kels! He murked Kels over that ho!"

They ran to the front breezeway and saw Kels lying slumped over on the stairs. Blood dripped down his body and a large red puddle had formed underneath the stairs.

Short Dogg knew he was dead even before he realized half of his face missing the right side.

Later that night after the police and detectives had left, the M.O.B. met at the spot. Everybody was saddened by Kels death. Even though Kels was a time bomb and hot head who stayed in some kind of altercation or another, he was one of theirs and the M.O.B. was gonna ride for him.

"My nigga, we ridin' for Kels," Short Dogg said, starting the meeting off. "That girl off limits. She didn't have shit to do with what went down. We fuck with some of them N.O. niggas and y'all know the ones we fuck with. Murk everythang else. Hit every apartment complex around this bitch and smoke everythang from the boot that ain't M.O.B. related or M.O.B. approved."

"Let's roll out, Lil Murda," Big Mack said to his partner in crime. Together, they would charge hell with a cup of spit.

***

That night, the streets of North Dallas ran bloody. Five people were murdered and there were twelve other shootings. For the next ten nights there was a murder. The

M.O.B. had declared war on niggas from the boot. The niggas from the boot loved that type of shit. Even though they were outnumbered and outgunned they fought back like true warriors. They fought back by robbing every spot they caught slipping.

Late one night, Short Dogg was standing outside the spot ducked off in the breezeway. He was on his cell phone talking to Zell, a white schoolteacher he had been spending more and more time with. He saw a late model Lincoln pull up and a chubby, dark skinned nigga got out of the car. The stupid nigga headed up the stairs and right over to where Short Dogg was standing without even noticing him. Short Dogg had also seen two other niggas in the car.

Ronnie had been sitting on the third floor selling bags of weed, so he thought nothing of it, since the weed spot had been rolling and niggas had been coming through all night. He could hear talking coming from up the stairs but paid it no mind.

Short Dogg kept on talking to Zell, telling her how he was going to tear that pussy up later on. All of a sudden, he heard the thunderous blast of a shotgun. Then, a second later, another blast.

"I'ma call you back," he told Zoe and quickly ended the call. Short Dogg pulled out his .45.

The dark skinned nigga came running down the stairs gripping a sawed-off shotgun. Short Dog unloaded on the nigga as soon as he made it off the steps, then he turned and unloaded on the two niggas in the Lincoln. He had a 17-shot clip in his .45.

"What the fuck you niggas thought this was?" Short Dogg yelled running up on the nigga he'd shot first.

Bloc! Bloc! Bloc!

"You dumb motherfuckers fuckin' with the M.O.B.!" He turned back to the car and ran up on the passenger side, repeatedly dumping shots into their dead bodies.

Bloc! Bloc! Bloc! Bloc!

"I'ma murk all you niggas!"

Bloc! Bloc! Bloc!

"This my block! I'm the king of Forest Lane, bitch niggas! Don't ever try to pull no shit like this on my block!" Short was so crunk he had snapped, never realizing he was talking to three dead bodies. He hadn't even noticed all the M.O.B. who had run outside.

Dub and Lil Chris walked over to him. "Chill, Big homie, them niggas dead but they slumped T-boy and Ronnie. What the fuck happened?" Chris asked.

"This lil bitch nigga," —Short Dogg said, as he walked over to the first nigga he'd slumped, and kicked him multiple times — "Got out the car and went upstairs. He must have had the shotgun under that trench" —he pointed to the bloody coat the dead man was wearing— "I was standing by the door and the nigga didn't even see me. I heard the nigga shoot T-Boy and Ronnie then he came running down ·the stairs. I domed his bitch ass then I wet them fuck niggas in the car."

"Blood, you gotta get outta here before the laws get here. Give me the gun," Dub said, taking the gun and firing a few rounds into the car. "Hop the gate and go to Shalika spot. I'ma tell the laws I did it. You a ex-con. Go ahead and dip. We got it."

Short Dogg took off running to Shalika's spot and called Zell to come pick him up. He spent the next two weeks laying low with her.

The police took Dub to the station but released him the next morning. The three niggas in the Lincoln had been wanted in three other robbery-homicides that had taken place in a six-hour time span.

After the incident, the management at the Bent Creek apartments evicted a lot of residents. They hired armed security guards to patrol the grounds twenty-four-seven, on foot, and they closed the back gate making the apartments one way in and one way out.

They built a security booth at the front gate with an armed guard inside who checked the names of anyone who tried to enter the apartment complex. The place that had been the headquarters of the M.O.B. was now shut down.

Chapter 8

"A penny for your thoughts," Zell said, as she curled up next to Short Dogg on the sofa. Her head rested on his shoulder.

"Money ... how to get it and how to keep it," he answered.

Zell was a thirty-four-year-old, shorter version of the country singer, Carrie Underwood. She taught fifth grade at Lake Highlands Middle School and had a half-Black fourteen-year-old daughter that Short Dogg loved and treated like his own.

Short Dogg had met Zell one night at a small neighborhood bar that he frequented often. It was a quiet, little duck-off spot where a lot of older people hung out. He liked to go there, have a few drinks, and just relax.

That particular night, he was chilling and enjoying the music while sipping on a shot of Patrón, and a Bud Light. The waitress had brought him over a fresh drink and beer and told him it was sent from the lady over at the pool table.

He looked over to where she pointed and saw a nice looking White woman in a pair of form-fitting blue jeans, a tank top, and heels. She waved him over and pointed to the pool table.

Damn, he thought as he got closer, she got a lot of ass for a White girl. After they introduced themselves to one another, they played a few games of pool, then sat down and talked the night away. Short Dogg found himself enjoying her company and becoming attracted to the soft-spoken White woman.

She had actually fallen in love with him in the short time they'd known each other. Even though she didn't think he was in love with her, and felt there were other females he was involved with, she was satisfied with whatever time he was willing to spend with her.

Lately, he had been spending more and more time with her and her daughter Danielle. Most mornings, he'd take Danielle to school and pick her up when she got out.

"Money can't make you happy," Zell responded.

"Maybe not completely happy, but it makes you happier than you'd be without it," he replied.

"Did somebody say something about money?" Danielle asked, entering the room. She sat on the other side of him and put her head on his other shoulder. "It would make me very happy," she said, in reference to money.

Short Dogg laughed and gave her a hundred dollar bill.

"Thank you," she said, and planted a kiss on his cheek. She smiled and pocketed the money.

"You spoil that girl too much," Zell said.

"Hater," Danielle whispered in his ear, and chuckled playfully.

"I heard that," Zell said.

Short Dogg laughed. "This is my baby girl. You already know, what Danielle wants, Danielle will get from me."

"Hey," Danielle said, giving him a high five.

She was a beautiful young girl and well-developed for her age. She was on the thick side with reddish brown hair and light brown eyes. She kind of reminded you of the singer Jordan Sparks. Short Dogg knew he was going to have to run a lot of lil niggas off real soon.

"Omar, are you taking me to school in the morning? I need to talk to you about something."

He knew it was about a boy. Lately, they had been talking about boys a lot. She would always tell him about her boy problems and ask for advice.

"I'll be here."

Zell was excited to learn that he'd be spending the night because she knew there was a pretty good chance she'd be getting some dick.

"Come on, Daddy, let's go for your walk," Short Dogg said to the pit bull he'd given them almost a year ago prior. He walked to the door and bent down and placed the leash around the dog's neck.

"You coming?" he turned around and asked Zell as he stood at the doorway.

"Sure, let me put on my shoe's," she said.

Short Dogg was five feet eight inches tall and Zell was five feet even. He was twenty-six years old and his body was all muscles from working out and lifting weights while he was in prison. He had light complexion and wore his hair in dreads that hung past his shoulders. Multiple tattoos decorated his body. He was a good-looking nigga who most females looked at twice.

As they walked outside, he took her hand and pulled her close. Leaning down, he met her lips with his and stuck a yard of tongue down her throat. At the same time, he grabbed her ass while pulling her closer, allowing her to feel his semi-hard dick against her stomach.

As they broke the kiss, a soft moan escaped her throat. "What was that for?" she asked.

"Just because."

"Because what?" she asked coyishly.

Before he answered, he thought back to how he had been feeling during the past couple of weeks while he'd been laying low at Zell's spot. He had slowly fallen in love with her. He knew how she felt about him and he knew in his heart she was a good woman. Even more, he knew he couldn't go wrong locking her down.

"I want you to be my woman. I'ma stop fightin' what I feel for you and what's been happenin' between us. I'm put a ring on your finger. The ring I'ma put on your finger makes it official that I'm your man and you my woman. You down with that?"

"Hell yes," she answered, breathlessly and taken aback.

"So look me in the eye and tell me you my woman.

"I'm your woman forever, 'til death do us apart."

"He took her hand and placed it over his heart and said, "You have my heart filled with joy right now. Don't do anything to fill it with hate."

"I promise. I'll never hurt you," she said, with tears in her eyes. He pulled her into him and they kissed for the longest time.

"Okay, that's law then. Let's hurry up with Daddy's walk so we can get back to the house so I can beat that pussy up," he said, letting her know he was planning on putting in some major work on that pussy.

He kissed her again while slipping his hand down the front of her sweatpants, then he rubbed his finger between her pussy lips in one smooth motion. He pulled his hand out and looked her in the eyes, then put the finger with her pussy juices on it in his mouth.

Zell almost fainted. She grabbed his hand and said, "Let's go home now." On the cool she loved it when he did that freaky shit to her. She had really fallen hard for him. He was a bad boy but he treated her with respect at all times. The small things he did, like running her bath water, getting her a drink, or even cooking sometimes, was what made her fall for him. He was really considerate and aware of her wants and needs. She felt safe and protected when she was with him. Not to mention the fact that he fucked her almost senseless.

Zell had only been in one relationship in her thirty-four years and that was with Danielle's father. They had been high school sweethearts and married straight out of high school.

He spent a year with her, enjoying their marriage before he went into the marines. Seven years later he was killed in an accidental explosion while serving in Iraq. She'd had a few lovers since Daniel's death but nothing serious. Before the first time Short Dogg fucked her brains out, she hadn't had sex in over a year and a half.

When he and Zell made it back, Daddy ran to his favorite spot and curled up. Danielle was asleep, so they showered together and for the first time since they'd had sex, Short Dogg went down on her and ate her pussy as if it was a plate of Oxtails.

Chapter 9

Short Dogg moved the headquarters to the Palms, where Shalika stayed. They were bigger and had more privacy than Bent Creek. The Palms were like mini condominiums. To avoid all the paperwork, he had to pay the manager fifteen hundred dollars to let him get an apartment.

The move went smoothly, but Lil Murda and Big Mack were still making the block hot. Their latest robbery had left a Mexican woman dead in a traphouse. The homicide detectives and undercover officers were all over the hood. It was hard to make any money.

Short Dogg got another apartment in the Estates off Abrams and 635 and it was on the edge of M.O.B. territory. A lot of New Orleanian niggas stayed or hung out in the Estates. A lot of them were jackboys and since Short Dogg had been moving a lot of work, he made sure B-Dub and Lil Chris stayed on their toes.

"Bro, this shit over with," Kim told him one day. She had come over to the new spot to put him up on some new moves she was making.

Kim was smart. The whole time her spots were rolling, she had been saving her money up, going to cosmetology school and learning how to do hair. She had all the girls in her circle doing the same thing.

"Lil Murda and my dumb ass brother, Big Mack, outta control. They not gon' stop 'til they locked up or dead. They don't even have their spots no more. They been let them go.

Now, all they do is rob dope houses and kill people. Them damn fools killed that Mexican girl the other day." She looked at Dogg and shook her head.

"I heard about that. Who was the girl?" he asked.

"You know the lil nigga, Money Mike, who had the spot in the Village?" She questioned him in an attempt to jog his memory, and when he nodded in the affirmative, she continued. "Well, they went to rob his spot and the girl answered the door with a gun in her hand and Lil Murda panicked and domed the bitch and ran off. They been hangin' with that nigga, Tip. The one who was with Kels when he got killed.

Murda Murda Murda Short Dogg had never really liked the nigga Tip because he always saw the nigga hanging with that fuck boy Bud and he knew those niggas were always on some snake shit.

"They killed three niggas in the Crossings about two or three weeks ago, then they turned right around and killed that fool in the Hallows. I couldn't make no money if I wanted to. I'm lettin' all my spots go at the end of the month. "I'm done, Bro. Me and my girls gon' open our first nail shop and beauty salon the first of the month. I got five spots opening in the next two months— two in Oak Cliff, two in the north and one in the Grove," Kim explained.

That's good, sis. I'm about to lay this shit down too. I been really thinkin' about marryin' Zell and gettin' outta the city … move out toward Prosper or something," he admitted.

"Boy, you lyin'," Kim said with increased volume, as she displayed her surprise. "That White girl done locked that dick down like that? Damn near every bitch on the Lane done tried that and you didn't give them hoes the time of day. As far as I know, Shalika 'bout the only bitch on the block who done got some of that dick. Bro, I gotta see that shit to believe it. You? married? Shiiit!" she said, shaking her head.

Short Dogg was laughing so hard he had tears falling from of his eyes. He and Kim had been like sister and brother ever since they'd first met.

"Nah, sis, that White woman just real. I can chill with her and let my guard down and not have to worry about no hidden motives or shit like that."

"I feel you, bro. I like Zell and I think she'll be good for you. But these bitches gon' be hatin' like a muthafucka," Kim said She knew all too well how females were.

As they sat around smoking and talking, he thought back to the first night he knew he had fallen for Zell. It wasn't long after Kel's funeral. He had been hanging out at the sports bar with Dub and Chris when Zell called him …

"Baby, are you busy?" he could hear panic and anger in her voice and his heart started racing immediately.

"Nah, what's wrong?"

"I was outside walking Daddy and that tall guy who's always hanging around started talking to me. Then, all of a sudden, he started talking crazy and nasty so I told him our conversation was over and started walking back to the house. The asshole grabbed my arm and Daddy tried to bite him but I held him back. He acted like he was going to attack me, and if Daddy hadn't been with me he probably would have."

"Where he at now?"

"He was still hanging around outside when I looked out the window to make sure he hadn't followed me to the door," Zell said.

"I'm on my way. Stay in the house and turn the lights on the back patio off," Short Dogg instructed her.

He went to his office and got an old throwaway 9 mm he had stashed before asking Lil Chris and B-Dub to roll with him, after he'd told them what was going on.

They rolled through Zell's complex but didn't see the fool. Short Dogg knew exactly who she was talking about. He was a smoker named Johnboy. They rolled by a couple more apartments until they spotted him sitting on the steps in one of the breezeways.

Short Dogg told Lil Chris to park the truck in the back of the apartments. He put his hoody on and slipped up behind him. When Johnboy turned around and saw Short Dogg, he knew he had fucked up. The look on his face said it all and Short Dogg told him before he unloaded the clip in his face and chest.

"You know you fucked up, right?"

Bloc! Bloc! Bloc!

Short Dogg ran back to the truck and Chris drove off spinning wheels. "Drop me off at Zell's and I'll get at y'all tomorrow." He hopped out of the truck and walked through the back gate and onto her patio. He sat down for a few minutes to calm his nerves and to replay everything that had taken place. He had to be sure he hadn't made any mistakes or left any loose ends that needed tying. He smoked a blunt and leaned back in the chair with his eyes closed.

Finally, he got up and knocked softly on the back door. He could hear Daddy scratching on the door before Zell opened it. As soon as she saw his face she fell into his arms crying.

"What you cryin' for, ma?"

"I was so scared."

"You don't have to worry about nothin'. I got you, alright?" he said, lifting her head up and kissing her on the lips.

"I really need to get out of these clothes, baby."

"Okay." She led him into their bedroom and undressed him. He pulled out the 9 mm, disassembled it, and wiped it off to remove any prints. Zell wiped each piece again with bleach and put them in a trash bag. She took his clothes to the washing machine and washed them.

Short Dogg watched her every move and said to himself, "Damn, that White woman solid and down as a muthafucka."

After they showered, they made love, and that was the first time he fucked her without a condom. That was the night Zell fell completely in love.

***

A few nights later, Short Dogg had just finished having dinner with Zell and Danielle when his cell phone rang. He looked at the screen and saw that it was Kim calling.

"What's up?"

"Where you at, bro? I need to holla at you and it's real important," Kim said.

"I'm at Zell's. Come on through. You by yourself?"

"I got Dub with me."

"Alright you good. Come on through," Short Dogg said, before hanging up. "Baby, Kim and Dub coming by for a few minutes. Can you put on somethin' over them tight ass boy shorts. I don't need my lil homie checkin' out my woman. Yo' pussy fat as a muthafucka in them boyshorts," he said, reaching over and rubbing between her legs.

"Ewww! Y'all so nasty," Danielle said, walking in the room.

"Nah, baby girl, that's not nasty. That's what you call being in love," Short Dogg told Danielle, while staring Zell down. He knew she loved it when he acted jealous and overly protective.

When Kim and Dub finally arrived, the news they brought with them tore a hole in his chest. Lil Chris had died a few hours before in a car accident as he was leaving his baby's mama's house. The suspected cause was alcohol.

Short Dogg, Lil Chris, Dub, D-money, and Bobi had all grown up in Oak Cliff together. Short Dogg was a few years older than them. He was their big homie. When he moved to the north, Lil Chris and Dub were out there almost every day hanging out with him. When they started hustling full time they both moved to the north with Short Dogg. Not long after, D-Money and Bobi also made the move.

He couldn't stop the tears that fell from his eyes. Zell sat on his lap and held his head against her chest. Seeing the pain and sorrow he was feeling made all of them break down too. Dub was in shock. He just sat there staring at the floor with tears running down his face.

Short Dogg called Lil Chris' mother, Mrs. Betty, and she told him Chris had spent the day with his kids and baby's mother. He'd had a few drinks but hadn't appeared to be drunk. On his way back to the north, his car hit the guard rail and flipped over. The police informed her that Chris had died instantly.

"I know how close you, Brandon, Jacoby, and D'yani were with Chris," she said, referring to Bobi and D-Money by their government names. "But don't y'all be over there feeling sad and crying for him. It was just his time to go and the Lord needed him in heaven to do some work up there, so he's at home with the Lord now. And Chris wouldn't want y'all to be sad and crying," she told him, in her usual motherly tone.

"Yes, ma'am, Mrs. Betty. I know you right but it's hard. Chris was our best friend since forever," Short Dogg said, choking up again.

"I know, Omar. You just have to trust in God and know He knows best. Now let me get off this phone before you have me crying again." Her pain was evident in her voice.

"Alright. I'm paying for the funeral so don't worry about that," Short Dogg said sincerely.

"Thank you, son. Call me later in the week and I'll have some details on the wake and funeral."

"Yes, ma'am. I will. You take care and I'll call you later, Mrs. Betty.

"You too, and thank you, Omar. Bye, son."

"Bye."

"Baby, I need a drink, Short Dogg said to Zell after he'd hung up the phone and regained his composure."

Zell went to the bedroom and got his weed box while Danielle went to the bar and got a bottle of Patrón and some cups. Kim rolled a blunt while Zell poured the drinks. Then, they got drunk and high and reminisced as they told stories about Chris all night.

"You remember Chris twenty-first birthday party at your brother Jay apartment?" Bud asked Short Dogg smiling.

"Hell yeah," he answered, laughing. "That nigga Chris got so drunk he passed out with his mouth wide the fuck open. Then, Jay and Glenn poured hot sauce, jalapeño pepper juice, and all kinds of hot shit in that nigga mouth." Short Dogg laughed as he recalled the night. "Baby, that nigga Chris jumped up hollerin', talkin' 'bout his mustache was on fire!" he said, looking at Zell. They burst out laughing.

"What about that time his baby mama caught him cheatin' with Suck Em' Up Tammy and chased that fool out the spot damn near naked and beatin' his ass with a broom stick?" Kim added.

"I had to go wrestle her ass down," Short Dogg said, laughing so hard he had tears in his eyes.

***

Big Mack was in the county jail on a federal charge with no bond for a pistol charge. When he called home, Kim told him about Lil Chris and he'd broken down so bad over the phone, it got to the point that he couldn't even talk anymore. He was upset he wouldn't be able to attend the candlelight vigil, the wake, or the funeral. He really wanted to be around his homies during a time when everyone was stressing and hurting over the death of one of their best friends. But two days before the funeral, the feds dropped the pistol charge and Big Mack was released.

They took him to the funeral home right before the funeral so he could pay his last respects to his departed homie. He stopped everybody at the door and asked them to let him get a few minutes alone with Chris. Ha didn't want the rest of the M.O.B. to see him break down and shed a few tears.

Lil Chris was buried in a red casket and dressed in a red Versace suit. Carnations, and red and white roses decorated the church beautifully. When Short Dogg walked up to the casket, he took off his chain and the M.O.B. pendant with the red diamonds and laid it across Lil Chris' chest.

They took donations for his three little girls and gave the money to Mrs. Betty. Lil Murda tore the church up when he got up and sang "Gangsta Lean" by DSR. The whole Lane and All the O.G.s from 22 Beckley were at the funeral. Short Dogg's mother, Pops, and all his brothers, and his sister were there as well.

Chapter 10

Andre "Big Dre" Williams was born and raised in Austin, Texas. He had been sentenced to twenty years in the Texas State Prison System for selling heroin; as a matter of fact, his whole family had sold heroin all his life. He could never get used to people telling him what to do and when to do it because it wasn't something he was accustomed to. Having to live in a small ass cell with another nigga had been what he'd despised the most. He had been incarcerated for seven years before being released on parole. He went back to Austin and vowed he would never go back to prison again. As such, he got a job making ten dollars an hour as a warehouse forklift driver. For a while, he had given up life as a drug dealer, that is, until he got a call from Short Dogg.

When he got to Dallas, Short Dogg gave him a hundred stacks and told him what he needed him to do, and just like that, he was back in the game. He called some of his old customers and told them he was back at it again with some top flight "H" for the low-low. They started putting in orders immediately because they knew he kept good product at reasonable prices.

Big Dre wasn't a damn fool. He knew the lick Short Dogg had hit would generate a lot of money. He also knew what kind of heat niggas who never had shit could bring. Especially once they started making that kind of money and spending it on expensive cars and jewelry. As well, he knew Short Dogg had put the young niggas on the set.

He'd met a lot of the niggas and knew most of them were damn fools who couldn't be trusted. So, with that in mind, Big Dre went back to Austin and got, what he called, his "insurance policy" back on his team.

Back when Dre was in the game, he had three bitches who moved most of his work for him— three straight up gangster bitches who were government-trained assassins.

Kelly "K-Rock" Simpson was from Flint, Michigan. A caramel complexioned Black woman, she stood five foot seven and weighed one hundred forty-five pounds. After she'd left the Army, she was recruited to Langley, Virginia. The Central Intelligence Agency had turned Kelly into a trained killer.

Sadly, while she was away, her entire family was murdered back in Flint, and having been trained to kill, she immediately retired and returned to her hometown to seek street justice. It didn't take her long to find the culprits responsible for her family's deaths, and when she did, she handled them all. Shortly after, she reunited with her best friends from the Army and relocated to Texas.

Michelle "Em" Turner was from Austin and she was one of Big Dre's childhood friend. Standing nearly six feet tall, she was athletic in stature and considered a pretty girl. Her tone dark-brown and as smooth as a Hershey's Kiss, and to say that her body was stacked would be an understatement. Like Kelly, she had also been in the Army, but she had been trained as a sniper and had also been a part of the bomb squad.

When she came home from the military and saw how Big Dre was getting money, she became part of his team and brought J-low with her. When K-Rock was done with family business, she eventually relocated to Texas and joined the team too.

Jasmine "J-low" Martinez was born in Phoenix, Arizona. She was a short Mexican girl who had attributes that resembled Eva Mendes. She had gone to the military straight out of high school. Her father had made her join the Army after she started hanging with the wrong crowd. She had been arrested for petty crimes and had gone to juvenile several times. Her and Em had worked on the bomb squad together. After leaving the Army, she followed her best friend to Texas.

"I need y'all to go to Dallas," Dre told them, as they sat during a meeting in his old apartment. "I'm back in the game. I got damn near three hundred bricks of pure heroin that ain't even been cut yet and I need to get it off. Once this work is gone, I'm retirin' for good. All of us gon' be rich after this, so don't go spendin' money like you ain't never had shit.

I'm helpin' my nigga get this work off 'cause the nigga like a brother to me. So, I need y'all to protect him like y'all would protect me, and I promise he gon' look out for all of us," he finished.

"When we leavin'?" Em asked, always ready to get to the bag.

"I need y'all to leave as soon as y'all can. I already got a three-bedroom condo for y'all. Matter of fact, y'all own it and it's already paid for," he told them. "Here go the deed," he said, handing the paper to Em. I'ma have my nigga meet y'all when y'all get settled in."

Dre brought three bricks that he planned to leave in Austin with a few of his homies to break down and sell in packs. He had made some moves with some of his old contacts and already had a white boy from Nebraska on his way to Dallas to get twenty-five bricks. Some niggas from Detroit were coming to score twenty and some people from New Mexico and Oklahoma were coming to score too.

He was going to get this money but he was also going to be prepared for any drama that happened to come his way. He was going to make sure that his nigga Short Dogg was protected at all times. He had a funny feeling shit was about to hit the fan with them M.O.B. niggas. He knew how money and jealousy could change niggas *and* bitches. He knew it wasn't all love like them niggas pretended it to be.

Chapter 11

Short Dogg and Danielle were riding in his new Range Rover headed to Prosper, a small town about an hour outside of Dallas. Dion Sanders, who once played for the Dallas Cowboys, had a ranch in Prosper. Short Dogg had purchased a huge eight bedroom, eight-and-a-half bathroom, brick house that sat on twenty-five acres. The property had a creek, electric gates, a six-car garage, an indoor swimming pool and a hot tub. Add to that a sunroom, two living areas, four fireplaces, a theater room, party room, and huge front and back decks.

"What is this place?" Danielle asked.

"You like it?" Short Dogg asked, as he opened the front door. They stood in the foyer with two sets of stairs leading to the second floor.

"Hell yeah, it's beautiful."

He reached into his pocket and pulled out a small box and handed it to her. She opened it and what she found was a beautiful, three-carat, diamond-and-platinum ring. She looked at him puzzled and asked, "What's this?"

"Is it alright with you if I ask your mom to marry me?" He asked for her blessings.

Danielle's eyes gleamed and her smile spread wide. "Hell yeah!" She answered without uncertainty.

"I bought this place for us. This is going to be our new home if she says yes."

"She'll say yes," she said confidently.

"How you know?"

"I knew her before she met you and she's never been this happy. Trust me, she'll say yes," she assured him.

"We gon' ask her tonight."

Short Dogg explained how he was going to propose and they spent the rest of the day planning everything and making phone calls. Then they went home to wait on Zell to get home   from her summer-school job.

When Zell returned home later that day, Short Dogg and Danielle were watching TV innocently, as if it were just a regular day.

"Hey, baby, how was your day?" he asked. He stood up and leaned in to give her a kiss, and he squeezed her ass impishly.

"It was okay. I have a nice group of kids this summer."

"Hey, Mom," Danielle said. She walked over and gave her mother a warm embrace.

"Hey, you."

"You didn't forget that we're going out tonight, did you?"

"No, I didn't forget. I'm going to get out of these clothes," she said. She turned and headed to her bedroom.

Short Dogg watched her as she walked out of the room and thought to himself, *damn baby ass fat in them slacks.* She was wearing an Alexander McQueen tan-colored pantsuit. He picked up his phone and sent her a text.

Short Dogg: You already got a nice ass but those pants got your ass jiggling and shaking every time you take a step. Damn, you fine! I wanna suck that pussy. You got my dick hard as a muthafucka. You in the mood for a quickie?

A few seconds later, his phone vibrated letting him know he had an incoming text. He looked at his phone and read the text.

Zell: Hurry, I'm already naked.

He hurried to the bedroom where he found Zell lying in the bed, rubbing her breast. "What took you so long?"

He undressed and started sucking her titties, causing her to moan in pleasure.

"You promised me some head," she said.

"I got you, baby," he said, running his tongue down her stomach and continued to her pussy. "Damn, baby, yo' pussy soaking wet," he told her, before he started licking her juices up.

"It's been like that all day. I need you inside me," she whispered.

"Hold on, baby, let me taste this pussy for a minute." He sucked on her pussy until she came hard, all over his face. She pulled him up and turned around and grabbed the edge of the bed.

"Beat it up," she said, guiding his dick inside her.

He banged her back out for almost an hour before they collapsed on the bed and fell into a deep sleep.

A few hours later, they woke up to Danielle banging on the bedroom door.

"Mom … Omar… Are y'all getting ready to go? It's already seven thirty.

"Damn, baby, we gotta hurry up," he said, getting up to head to the shower. You comin' in here with me?"

"Yeah, I'm comin'."

***

He let Zell drive. He put the address in the navigation system and she followed the directions. As they got closer to their destination he sent a text to his mother letting her know they were about ten minutes away.

When they pulled up Zell looked at the house and said, "It's beautiful." He had already told her he wanted her to look at a house he was thinking about buying.

With the help of his mother and Pops, they had set up a small table in the front entryway that had three chairs and a bottle of champagne chilling on ice. In the back room, several family members and friends of his and Zell's were waiting to celebrate the proposal— *if* she said yes. There were also caterers on the way.

They walked inside and she saw the table with the chairs, the candles, and the champagne.

"What is this?" Zell asked puzzled.

"Sit down right here for a minute. Danielle, you sit down over there, right next to your mother," he said, and pointed to the chair. He opened the bottle and poured them each a glass. He only filled Danielle's halfway.

"Hell yeah!" Danielle said, reaching for her glass.

After they had taken sips of their champagne, he sat his glass down, dropped to one knee and took Zell's hand in his.

"Zell, in the past two years I have gotten to know you and Danielle, and I know that I don't want to go another day without knowing you'll be in my life forever. I love you, Zell," he said. He reached in his pocket and pulled out the ring—"Will you be my wife?"

"Oh my God, yes, yes, yes," she answered, with tears streaming down her face. She jumped in his arms, and they shared a long kiss.

"Ewww," Danielle said.

"Hold on, baby," he said. He put Zell down and turned to Danielle. "Babygirl, you already know how I feel about you and your mom. But I gotta ask you, will you be my daughter?" he asked, taking her hands.

"Hell yeah!"

He reached in his pocket and pulled out a set of keys and gave them to her. "Go look on the side of the house."

She took off running. He'd just given her the keys to a brand-new Chrysler 300.

"Come on, baby. There's a gang of people in the back waiting for us. When he opened the door to the theater room everyone yelled, "Congratulations!" And the party was on.

Big Dre, George and his girl Kwanta, Faye and Pops, all of his brothers, a few of Zell's friends, Dub, Bobi, and D-Money were all there to celebrate.

"Come over here, Omar," Faye said, calling her son over to where she and Pops were sitting, sipping on champagne. "Boy, I'm so proud of you. Zell is a beautiful woman, and she makes you happy. That's what counts… you being happy. I hope y'all have a long, wonderful marriage."

"Thank you, momma. I wish Chris was here with us," he said, giving her a hug and kiss on the cheek.

"He's here, and he's watching us right now," she reassured him.

"You did good, Son. That white woman bad," Pops said.

"Thanks, Pops," Short Dogg said.

His phone vibrated in his pocket letting him know he had received a text message. He pulled it out and saw that he had a text from Zell. He opened the text.

Zell: I'm waiting on you in our new bedroom.

He smiled and said, "Uh, excuse me Mom and Pops. I'll be right back," He hurried out of the room and took the stairs two at a time.

He walked in the bedroom and found Zell standing in the middle of the room with her eyes closed.

"What's up, baby? Why are you up here all alone?"

"I just wanted to take a look at the rest of the house and thank you for making me the happiest woman in the world. I love you, Omar, and I'm going to be so proud to wear your last name," she said kissing him.

"I love you too, baby, and I have never wanted anyone else to have my last name but you."

"We need to christen our new bedroom," Zell whispered in his ear.

"What you mean, baby?"

"I want to give you a blow job," Zell said. She reached down and unzipped his pants.

"You ain't said shit," he said, helping her get his dick out.

She licked the head a few times then she pulled his nuts out and sucked each one, before she ran her tongue up one side, and down the other side of his dick. She looked up at him before she swallowed his whole dick.

"Damn, baby …. you eatin' the fuck outta that dick."

She was slurping, smacking, and moaning all at the same time. She went into a zone trying to get the nut out of his dick. Omar was in a zone from the sensations he was feeling from Zell's bomb ass head. Neither one of them heard the bedroom door open.

As soon as he started nuttin' they heard Danielle say, "Ewww, Mom, y'all nasty," she said, and slammed the door.

"Oh shit," he said, trying to pull his dick out of Zell's mouth.

But she grabbed his ass and pulled him deeper into her mouth. She didn't let him go until she had milked his dick dry.

"Baby, Danielle saw us," Short Dogg told her.

"She's sixteen, so I'm sure she knows what couples do. Next time she'll knock," Zell said.

The newly engaged couple left the room and went back downstairs to be hosts to their guests.

Chapter 12

Short Dogg had less than thirty days before his wedding day. He had already told Dub and the rest of the M.O.B. that he would be out of the game in the next couple of weeks. Basically, he had already turned over his spots to Dub, D-Money, and Bobi. He still had money coming in from the work he'd given Big Dre and all of his legal businesses. He was focused on building a family with Zell and Danielle.

One morning, not long after he'd proposed, he'd gone into the bathroom with Zell and noticed that she'd been taking a pill every morning before going to work. Later, after she was gone, he went and read the bottle and realized they were birth control pills.

The next morning, he made sure he went into the bathroom with her. When she opened the medicine cabinet and took out the bottle he took her hand before she could take the pill. He looked her in the eyes. "Baby, can we get rid of these?" he asked.

With tears in her eyes she nodded and flushed them down the toilet.

"Why you cryin'?" he asked, wiping her tears away.

"I've wanted to have your babies so bad but I just didn't know how to bring the subject up. We've never discussed having kids so I didn't know if it what you wanted," she answered honestly.

"I want you to have my babies. You don't gotta be scared or shy to talk to me about nothin'. Ah'ight?"

She nodded and they shared a long, passionate kiss. He reached into her panties to find her clit. "Damn, your pussy soaking wet," he said, pulling his hand out of her panties and licking her juices off his fingers.

"You do that to me every fuckin' time I'm around you," she said. She pulled his dick out and bent over the sink. They made love all over the bathroom before she jumped in the shower and hurried off to work.

***

Zell had been doing a lot of online shopping, for furniture for the new house. Short Dogg had gone online and found some African art that he'd purchased. Zell owned her townhouse, so she was going to rent it out as soon as they moved into the new home.

They were on their way to the house to meet the movers who were delivering some of the new things they'd ordered when Short Dogg's phone rang. He didn't recognize the number but answered anyway.

"Hello?"

"Is this Omar Wilson?"

"Yeah, who is this?" he questioned the caller.

This is homicide detective, Ben Pollard. I'm trying to get in touch with Roderick Miller. Your number was on one of his old bond papers.

Short Dogg knew Roderick Miller was Big Mack's government name. I'm not around him right now."

"If you can, will you tell him to give me a call whenever you see him. It's very important that I talk to him soon."

"I'll pass the message as soon as I see him."

"Okay. You know what this is about?" the detective asked.

"No," Short Dogg replied. "Well, I dropped those federal firearm violations against Roderick in return for his assistance in finding me some witnesses who'll testify against the guy who killed Kelly Johnson in the Bent Creek Apartments. Anyway, we arrested him two weeks ago in Tacoma, Washington," Detective Pollard explained.

"Yeah, well, I don't know nothin' about that, but I'll pass the message on and have him call you."

"Okay, thank you," the detective said, before hanging up.

"What's wrong?" Zell asked. She could clearly see the confused look on Short Dogg's face.

"A homicide detective lookin' for Big Mack. *So that's how he got outta jail on the federal no bond,* Short Dogg thought to himself. "Stop lookin' so worried. Everything ah'ight. He just wanna to talk to him," he told her. He reached over and rubbed her thigh. On the cool, he let his hand brush up against her pussy as she drove.

They got to the house and Zell became engrossed with the delivery people who had brought the furniture. Short Dogg used the opportunity to excuse himself. He found a quiet spot and called Big Mack's number. When didn't get an answer, he called Kim and told her to schedule a meeting for the O.G.s later on that night at the club.

After the phone call, he helped Zell with the furniture and made sure the house would be decorated the way she wanted it. He told her that even though she would be the one decorating the house, he was going to decorate the theater room because that was going to be his mancave where he entertained his brothers and homies.

He'd ordered two pool tables, an 80-inch flat screen, a twenty-four-piece sectional sofa, chairs and tables, plus there was already a built-in bar that he planned to stock with all the name-brand liquors. He also had several smaller televisions mounted on the walls so they could watch several different programs at once.

As he sat back and watched Zell organize things and order the delivery men around, he thought to himself, *I got a bad ass woman.* He smiled as he watched her direct the men as to where to place a particular piece of furniture, then five minutes later, she'd change her mind and have them move it someplace else. She'd bought a lot of the furniture with her own money without even telling him.

Her mother and father owned a trucking company with ten trucks that transported merchandise all over the United States, Canada, and Mexico. Her father had passed away over ten years ago and she had inherited half of the company. Her mother remarried and her and her new husband drove one of their eighteen wheelers and traveled state to state and city to city seeing the world. They practically lived on the road. Zell didn't really associate with her mother's husband because he'd made a comment about Danielle being half-black and questioned Zell's preference for Black men. She wasn't even going to invite her mother to the wedding.

Damn she fine, Short Dogg thought as he continued watching her. She was wearing a pair of blue jean shorts, a tank top, and a cute pair of casual sandals showed off her petite feet. She had a bubble butt and wide hips. Her legs made his mouth water and her thighs were big and firm. Every pair of pants or shorts she put on seemed to find their way up the crack of her ass, and her ass jiggled every time she moved. *Damn, I'm sittin' here with a hard on,* he thought, as he moved his dick around in pants to prevent the tent that had formed. *I'ma fuck the shit outta her as soon as these muthafuckas leave.* He pulled his phone out and sent her a text.

Short Dogg: You got a beautiful ass I can't wait 'til these people leave.

He saw her pull her phone out, look at it, and smile. Then she looked at him from across the room, turned, and bent over as if she was picking something up from the floor. She looked back and winked. The way Omar looked at her made her horny.

"Okay, guy's, that's enough for today, but we'll pick up where we left off tomorrow," she said trying to hurry them out of the door.

As they were leaving, he gave each one of them a fifty-dollar tip. By the time he had closed and locked the door, Zell had disappeared. He looked everywhere but couldn't find her downstairs anywhere. He ran up the stairs and found her in their bedroom naked, and lying in the middle of their new bed rubbing her clit.

"Oh shit," he said removing his clothes in haste. "I'm finna fuck the shit outta you, baby."

"Talk is cheap," she said lustfully.

Chapter 13

At about ten o'clock, Short Dogg pulled up at the club he his little brother, Junior, owned. He went through the back door with his key and went straight to the office.

"What's up, Junior?"

"What up, Big Bro."

"Same old shit. What you got goin' on tonight?"

"Not much. Countin' this bread from last night."

"I'm about to go out here and make my rounds and see what's jumpin'. I'll catch up with you a little later on," he said, before leaving the office and going out to the club area.

The first people he saw were Dub and Kim.

"What y'all got goin' on?" he asked, locking up with them.

"Chillin'," Kim said.

"Everybody here?" he asked.

"Everybody except Murda and Mack," Dub answered.

"I'm finna walk around and see who up in this bitch tonight."

"You good if I take Dub with me, Kim?"

"Yeah, y'all go ahead. I'ma sit here and get me another drink."

"Ah'ight, let's roll, Dub."

They walked around and spoke to different patrons. He saw his boys Nine-fo and Pac Man who he hadn't seen in a long time. They had just been found not guilty on a murder charge and had been laying low. He nodded to them and got one of the waitresses to take them a bottle on the house.

They made their way to the VIP section where Short Dogg had his own roped off section. He saw a couple of people he hadn't seen in a minute and went over to talk to them.

"What's up?" he asked giving each one dap. "I ain't seen y'all in a minute. How that college life treatin' you?" he asked Todd.

"It's all good."

"What you up to, Rudy?"

"Same old, same old. Tryna stack a dollar," Rudy answered, letting Short Dogg know he was still pushing them bricks for the low-low.

Rudy was a Mexican whose family had connections to the cartel. Todd was a half-black, half Asian nigga who had dated a girl named Sharonda at the same time Short Dogg had been dating her older sister, Yolonda. Todd wasn't in the game. His family was practically rich, but he and Rudy had been friends since elementary.

"I'm gettin' married next weekend. I'm out the game and strictly gettin' that legal paper now," Short Dogg told him.

"That's good, and smart too. Stack your paper and get the fuck outta the way before the Feds come knockin'," Rudy said.

"Y'all be easy. Let me go holla at my young nigga," Short Dogg said, before making his way over to where Dub was sitting. He grabbed a seat ran down what the homicide detective had told him.

"Man, that nigga foul," Dub said.

I' m 'bout to let everybody know what the nigga up to. Let's go see if these niggas showed up yet."

When they made it to the front, Big Mack and Lil Murda were just walking through the door, so everyone headed toward the back where the conference room located.

There were five of them in the room. Big Mack, Lil Murda, Kim, Fred, and Short Dogg. Rob had moved back to Louisiana and Ronnie had been killed in the Bent Creek shooting.

The minute everyone was seated. Short Dogg immediately confronted Big Mack.

"Mack, what the fuck you got goin' on?"

"What you mean, Dogg? We ain't had shit to do with them niggas gettin' hit up at the corner store."

"Nigga, a homicide detective called my phone lookin' for you and told me he let you outta jail on that gun charge 'cause you agreed to get some witnesses to testify on the nigga who shot Kels."

"Yeah, so what? Fuck that nigga."

"Fuck you mean, nigga? That's snitchin'. We handle shit in the streets! We don't fuck with the police!"

"Fuck that nigga, homie! That nigga killed my nigga so whatever he get, he get."

"Nigga, we smoke niggas! We M.O.B., nigga! We don't put the laws on nobody. How many niggas have you killed? Them niggas had homies too but they ain't tell the laws on you. They tryna handle this shit in the streets, that's why you can't leave the house without a gun," Short Dogg said.

"Bro," Kim interrupted, "Big Mack didn't tell the laws shit. I'ma get some of them lil bitches to testify on the nigga."

"So the plot thickens. You down with this shit too, Kim?"

"Bro, you trippin'. Fuck that nigga! We M.O.B., she answered.

"Nah, y'all trippin'! Fuck that nigga! This ain't about him. This about y'all workin' with the police. One of us should'a kill that fuck nigga, not send him to jail. Nigga, I been locked in one of those cells and I don't wish jail on my worst enemy. How many of y'all was down with this?" Short Dogg asked, looking around the room. "Lil Murda, you knew about this shit?"

"I didn't know shit. This the first I heard about this shit. But I'm with Mack and Kim on this. Fuck that nigga."

"And what about you, Fred?"

"Don't insult me, blood. You know I ain't with this kinda of bullshit," Fred said.

"Y'all niggas got the game fucked up. I hate the police. Shit, if a nigga killed my mama I wouldn't put the laws on him. I'd murda er'thang the nigga love until I could murda him. I'm outta here, man. I don't want shit to do with nothin' y'all got goin' on," Short Dogg said, and headed to the door.

"Hold up, blood, I'm leavin' with you," Fred said, as he stood up. "Y'all trippin', and the fucked-up part about the whole situation is that y'all know y'all playin' a dirty game and can't even admit it and keep it gangsta. We kill snitches where I'm from. So I for damn sure ain't 'bout to roll with no police ass niggas," Fred added, before closing the door.

Chapter 14

Short Dogg stood at the altar in the backyard of their new home with Dub standing at his side as his best man. Handsome and debonair, he was dressed in a gray Ralph Lauren tux with a red shirt, gray tie, and black alligator shoes. Zell was draped in a white-and-red Vera Wang gown. As he watched Pops walk Zell down the aisle, his breath caught in his throat from the sight of her beauty. Her hair was curled and the blonde highlights seemed to make the strands shimmer under the sunlight. She had very little makeup on, but the pink lip gloss she was wearing had Short Dogg ready to kiss her before they said "I do".

Faye wouldn't let them spend the night together and she'd made Zell spend the night with her. However, the two lovebirds had stayed on the phone all night on FaceTime. It had been over twenty-four hours since he had touched her and he couldn't stand it.

When she'd made it down the aisle and stood before him, he reached out and took her hand. "You killin' that dress. You look so beautiful," he told her.

"Thank you."

The preacher did his thing and when it was time for Short Dogg to say his vows, he looked her in the eyes and said, "I can't even put into words what I feel for you, so I just want you to listen to this and I hope it says what my heart feels. Play it, Junior," he turned and said to his little brother. The song "Never" by Jahiem blared from the speakers.

Danielle was standing next to her mother and both women had tears in their eyes.

"Why you cryin'?" he asked Zell.

"These are tears of joy because you make me so damn happy," Zell answered.

"What are you crying for, babygirl?" he asked Danielle.

"Thank you for making my mom so happy. It's just been us for so long, and even though she tried to hide it, I could see how lonely she was until you came along. She's been a good mother and she deserves to be happy."

He had to grab Danielle and hug her so nobody would see the tears in his eyes. The three of them embraced one another in group hug and stayed that way until the preacher cleared his throat and broke up their moment.

"Zell, do you take Omar to be your lawfully wedded husband, to love and cherish until death do you part?"

"I do," she said.

"Omar, do you take Zell as your lawfully wedded wife to love, cherish and protect, until death do you apart?"

"I do."

"I now pronounce you man and wife. You may kiss the bride."

"Don't be shy. I want some of that tongue," he whispered in her ear.

"Not in front of Mama Faye," she answered.

"Boy, what is y'all up there whispering about? Kiss that girl so we can cut this cake," Faye said.

"You heard her," he said, and kissed her long and hard. He reached down, grabbed a handful of her ass, and pulled her into him, as their tongues did the French tango.

"Omar, let that girl's ass go in front of all these people," Faye said.

"Ewww, y'all nasty," Danielle said, which caused everyone to laugh.

Junior played "Spend My Life" by Eric Benet and Tamia then "Suffocate" by J. Holliday came on. When "Must Be

Nice" by Lyfe Jennings rang out, Zell and Short Dogg danced.

I wanna fuck the shit outta you while you wearin' that dress," he told her as they danced.

"I want you too," she admitted.

"Meet me upstairs in ten minutes. I'ma dance with my momma then I'm on my way," he said, before going over and pulling Faye out of her chair so they could dance.

"I'm happy for you, baby. I see how much you love that girl and I see how much she and Danielle care for you. Y'all gonna have a wonderful, happy marriage. But don't you mess over that girl by being out there in them streets chasin' them good-for-nothin' tramps," Faye warned him.

"I'm not even on nothin' like that. That white woman makes me very happy. I don't even think about no other women. She a fool in the bedroom." He laughed.

"Shut yo' nasty ass up, boy," Faye said, joining in the laughter. Get yo' nasty butt on 'cause I saw Zell sneak in the house a few minutes ago. What y'all tryna do? Sneak and get a quicky? Gone before everybody start payin' attention."

"Momma, I love you. You straight gangsta."

"You damn skippy, I am. I'm off Deuce Deuce Beckley," Faye said throwing up the set.

Short Dogg hurried in the house still laughing at his mother. When he got upstairs, Zell had pulled her dress up over her hips and was bent over the dresser, ass tooted, fingering herself.

"Damn, ma, you ain't have no panties on?" he asked, quickly pulling his pants below his hips.

"Of course not. I've been waiting on this all night."

"Shit, this pussy is wet," Short Dogg said, sliding inside her.

"Yes, it is … punish it, baby," she moaned.

He grabbed her hips and started fucking her long and hard. The gushy sounds coming from her pussy's wetness were driving him nearly insane.

"Baby, this pussy so good! Ma, this my pussy?"

"Yes, oh yes, it's yours. Don't stop, baby. Your dick is so fuckin' good," Zell said, throwing it back, matching him stroke-for-stroke. "I'm cummin', Omar. Oh shit, I'm cummin'," she moaned. Hot cum squirted out of her pussy for the first time in her life; so much so, it soaked his pants and thighs.

"Fuck, I'm nuttin' too," he yelled, shooting jets of cum inside her pussy.

They stayed like that until their heartbeats calmed. When he pulled out of her, she began to squirt again. "Oh shit, I'm cummin' again… put it back in," she screamed, as the most intense orgasm she'd ever had in her life rocked her body.

Finally satisfied, they allowed their bodies to separate. Zell turned around and realized his pants were drenched.

"Oh shit, I'm so sorry I ruined your pants.

"Fuck these pants. You don't have to ever apologize for wetting me up like that. That shit was the bomb," he said. before going into the bathroom. He grabbed a towel and wet it with warm water and soap before cleaning him and wifey up. He changed into some jeans and a T-shirt and the bride and groom went back downstairs holding hands.

Chapter 15

"Man, fuck that nigga. That nigga don't run shit. We all M.O.B. I wanna murk the nigga for playin' me close like that," Big Mack said, as him, Kim, Lil Murda, and Fred sat in Shalika's living room having a meeting on how to handle the situation with Short Dogg.

"I'm down for whatever. I don't give a fuck," Lil Murda added. Truth be told, he was still fucked up over the ass whooping Short Dogg had put on him.

"I'm thinkin' along those same lines. The nigga gotta be eliminated. If you ain't with us then you against us, and we can't stand for no shit like that to exist. We made that clear when we started the M.O.B. That nigga goin' against us for a nigga who killed one of ours," Kim said.

"I'm not 'bout to let my brother go down when we can trade that fuck nigga for one of our own. I don't see why that nigga Short Dogg can't see that. Yeah, it's dirty but the game dirty. So if a nigga ain't willin' to get dirty he need to get the fuck outta the game, you feel me?" Kim asked.

"I feel that," Mack answered.

"Me too," Lil Murda concurred.

"What you think, bro?" she asked Fred.

For a minute, Fred just sat there smoking his blunt and staring at them as if they had suddenly grown two heads. Then, he blew out a cloud of smoke and said, "I think y'all some damn fools. All y'all drivin' hundred-thousand-dollar cars and sittin' on thousands of dollars. The big homie made that happen. Kim, you know damn well them two niggas," he said pointing at Big Mack and Lil Murda with his blunt, "been outta control. Just last week you was tellin' me how they out here runnin' around the block robbin' and killin' and makin' the hood hot.

Just like blood said, every nigga you done shot or killed had a brother or some homeboys. But they didn't put the laws on you. We murk niggas, we don't fuck with the police. Kim, you know better than that. I been locked in a cell before so I would never send a nigga to jail or prison. Blood, go do your time like the standup nigga you 'pose to be and fuck the rest of the bullshit. That's what I think," Fred finished.

"Fuck what you talkin' about. I ain't puttin' myself in the penitentiary for nobody," Big Mack said.

"Well, I'm outta here," Fred said and got up to leave. "Just know if y'all go at the big blood y'all goin' at me too."

"Fuck you then, nigga," Big Mack yelled, as he jumped up, pulled out his pistol, and shot Fred three times in the face.

Bloc! Bloc! Bloc!

Knocking over a table and lamp, Fred fell to the floor. Then like a deranged lunatic, Lil Murda jumped up, pulled his strap, and shot into Fred's body three more times.

Shalika ran to the living room from her bedroom where she'd been listening to the meeting. "Why the fuck y'all doing that shit in my house? Look at all that blood on my shit!"

"Shut the fuck up," Big Mack yelled while pointing his gun at her. Lil Murda jumped in front of her and started to lift his pistol at Big Mack.

"What the fuck is you doin'?" Kim yelled at Big Mack and stepped in between all three of them. "Y'all put them muthafuckin' guns up. Nigga, Shalika family! If you ever pull some shit like that again, brother or not, I'ma pop you my muthafuckin' self!" she scolded him.

"I fucked up, that's my fault, Shalika. I was in a zone and at the same time you ran out here screamin' and I felt like you was a threat. I apologize," Big Mack said, not even realizing his main man, Lil Murda, would pop him before he'd let him hurt Shalika. He hadn't even noticed Murda lift the gun at him.

"Now, is everybody good in this bitch?" Kim asked, looking around from one face to another. She had seen the stunt Lil Murda had just pulled and thought to herself, *I'ma have to get rid of that niggaMurda 'cause the nigga clearly too weak over pussy.* He damn near smoked his ace over a bitch he hadn't even fucked yet and one who didn't even want him.

"Hell nah, we ain't good. Look at all this blood and there's a dead body in my damn living room!" Shalika said.

"Chill, I got this shit. In an hour you won't even know this shit happened," Mack said.

"Why the hell you do this shit in my house?"

"We couldn't let the nigga leave. He knew too much and the nigga wasn't down with us," Mack said.

"He right, Shalika. We couldn't let that nigga leave," Kim added. "Bro, y'all get this shit cleaned up. I'm finna take Shalika with me and get her outta here. She don't need to be involved in this shit."

"I'm already involved. They killed him in my house."

Don't nobody know that but us, so if you keep your mouth closed, nobody will ever know," Kim told her.

"I ain't sayin' shit!" She lied. "I just want that body and that blood outta my house."

"Just go with Kim, and we gonna clean this shit up," Lil Murda said. "Y'all go 'head and bounce. We got it. Come on, Murda, and help me carry this nigga to the tub 'til we get ready to move him up outta here."

After Kim and Shalika left, Big Mack and Murda moved all the furniture to the other rooms and bleached anything that could possibly have blood splattered on it, then they pulled the carpet up. Next, they went outside and got a crackhead, known on the streets as P-Diddy, and paid him to go into one of the vacant apartments and take the carpet out of *that* living room to put it in Shalika's living room, in place of the bloody carpet.

MurdaAfter that was done, they wrapped Fred's body in the bloody carpet and waited until it got dark before carrying the body to Big Mack's truck. They drove to South Dallas and took the body out of the carpet and left it in a vacant field. They then drove to another location in Oak Cliff and burned the bloody carpet.

"See, that's that gansta shit, big homie," Lil Murda said.

"Now, let's go hit them niggas' spot up in the Palms," Big Mack looked at him and responded.

"Let's go put this murda game down then. This the shit I live for right here," Lil Murda boasted.

When Shalika finally made it back to her apartment that night, she was surprised to see that there wasn't any evidence of Fred's murder. She tried calling Short Dogg again. She had been calling him every chance she got a moment away from Kim, unfortunately, he hadn't answered. Finally, he picked up.

"What's up Shalika?"

"Short Dogg," she said, and burst into tears," something happened, and I need to see you."

"Slow down and tell me what happened."

"Fred, baby … he gone. I don't want to tell you about it over the phone."

"I'm on my way. You at home?"

"No! Don't come over here. It ain't safe. I'll meet you somewhere."

"Ah'ight, meet me in the student parkin' lot of your old high school in one hour."

"Okay," she answered, before hanging up.

Short Dogg pulled up thirty minutes early. He called Shalika and told her he was there. She pulled up fifteen minutes later, parked, and got inside his truck with him. He put the truck in drive and pulled off.

"Baby, they killed Fred in my apartment."

"Who did, and when?"

"Lil Murda and Big Mack. Mack was about to shoot me too, but Murda and Kim jumped in front of me and made him put the gun down," she explained. She began to cry again.

"Start from the beginning and tell me what happened," he probed further.

"Kim was at my house when Lil Murda and Big Mack showed up. Then, they called Fred and told him to come over. They started talkin' about killin' you, and Fred told them if they got at you they would have to get at him too. Out of nowhere, Big Mack jumped up and shot him. Even after he was already on the floor dead, Murda put more bullets into his dead body."

"You sure he dead?"

"He dead, baby. They shot him multiple times in the face and the head."

"Where they at now?"

"I don't know… me and Kim left so they could clean up all the blood and get rid of the body. When I got back home they were gone. Short Dogg, don't trust Kim … she's behind all of this, baby."

"So she was down with them niggas talkin' 'bout killin' me?"

"Yes … she cosigned that shit and told them you had to go." Shalika told him straight up.

"Shalika, I'ma need you to do something for me. Let me make a few moves and I'ma call you later— from a different number though. Just play your roll if they come back and I'ma talk to you later," he told her coolly. He pulled back up to her car and parked.

"Can I suck that dick before I go?" she asked. She massaged his dick through his pants.

"Hurry up, Shalika. We out here in the school parking lot. Shit, the laws might roll through this bitch at any time."

She pulled his dick out, and in no time, she had him nuttin' down her throat. She swallowed hard and licked her lips as if it was the best thing she'd ever tasted.

"Be careful, Short Dogg, 'cause these niggas ain't playin' fair," she warned him, as she opened the door to get out of his truck.

He rolled his window down and eyed her intensely. "*You* be careful," he said in a stern tone.

"I will. Call me later," she said, and jumped back in her car.

Short Dogg drove off and immediately called his brothers. He explained what was going on and told them to stay woke. He made sure to tell Junior to stay away from the club until after the situation was resolved. Junior was angry about that but agreed to let the assistant manager run the club for a few days. He also told all the workers at the club to call him if they saw Kim, Big Mack, or Lil Murda at the club, or anywhere else in the hood.

He drove around in the hood for a few hours looking for Big Mack or Lil Murda. He knew Kim wouldn't be out, or at least he didn't think she would. He thought about going over to her house, knocking on her door, and blowing her whole head off. Nevertheless, he knew she would have six or seven bitches at her spot, and that was way too many witnesses.

Eventually, his stomach started calling his name so he called Zell and asked her if she and Danielle wanted to go out to get something to eat. They welcomed the invitation so he called it a night and made his way to pick them up.

Chapter 16

Dub, Bobi, D-Money, and the rest of the crew were chilling at the spot in the Palms. It was Friday night and the spot was rolling off the chain. They had already made over fifty stacks in less than ten hours.

"Y'all niggas ain't hungry?" Dub asked. He lit up a fat ass blunt of Kush.

"Hell yeah, you gonna go get something to eat?" D-Money asked.

"Slime, what's up? You wanna run up to Wing Stop and get some wings and shit?" Dub asked his lil nigga. Slime was playing Madden with the rest of the homies.

Slime was a nineteen-year-old hustler they had brought with them from Oak Cliff to get money. He wasn't M.O.B. but he was Deuce Deuce, and since M.O.B. was under the Deuce, he rode with the big homie, Short Dogg.

A tall and slim nigga with light skin, everybody called Slime a pretty boy. He was tatted up and kept a pair of flyy ass glasses on his face. Slime was like a little brother to Dub, and Dub had just helped him get his first car. A brand-new Range Rover right off the showroom floor. He'd left the car lot and went straight to the rim shop and got twenty-eight-inch shoes on his shit. Then he went to Car Toys and had the inside of his ride freaked out. He had twelve screen players, 3 twenty-five-hundred-watt amp system, an Xbox, 8 twelve-inch speakers, and the complete hook up was made by Bose.

He loved driving his truck, so when they asked him to go get the food he was more than happy to go.

"Stop by the corner store and get five packs of blunts on your way back too," Bobi said before he walked out the door.

When he got outside in the parking lot he saw a white Crown Victoria coming his way. He thought it was another customer coming to score until the car got right up on him and the two back doors flew open. Like characters out of the movie Scarface, Murda and Big Mack jumped out busting.

Slime was caught completely off guard and he was hit five times before he fell behind his truck. He heard the car burn rubber as it pulled off.

Everyone inside the spot heard the gunshots at the same time, and it sounded like a war was going on outside. They grabbed their guns and ran outside.

At first no one saw anything. Then as Bobi walked toward the Range Rover he saw Slime's red Polo boots sticking out from the side of the truck.

"Slime got hit," he said, running over to where his body lay. "Look at all that blood," he added, pulling out his phone to call 9-1-1.

"9-1-1, what is your emergency?

My homeboy just got shot," he told her in loud tone, "we need an ambulance, fast."

"What is your location, sir?"

"We at the Palms Apartments on Forest Lane, in the back parking lot."

"An ambulance is on the way. Can you stay on the line until they arrive?"

"Nah, I gotta help my homeboy," he said, hanging up the phone.

"Everybody get them guns off you before the laws get here," Dub said.

They took their guns and put them in Dub's car, which was parked right next to Slime's trunk, just in case the shooters came back.

Slime was still breathing and conscious. He was in a lot of pain because all of the bullets had hit him in his chest and stomach areas.

"Who did this shit?" Dub asked him.

"Lil Murda and that bitch nigga Big Mack. Them niggas got me dog. My stomach on fire. Hey blood, that bitch Kim was drivin' the car they got out of."

"You sure you saw Kim?" Bobi asked.

"Yeah, it was Kim."

"Where the fuck the ambulance at?" D-Money yelled.

A crowd had formed around them after hearing the gun shots. Everyone stood around talking about what they had seen, which direction the car had gone in, and what kind of car it had been.

"Hey!" Dub yelled to the crowd, "we don't talk to the police around here. Ain't nobody seen shit."

Finally, the police and the ambulance got there, loaded Slime on a stretcher, and took him straight to the hospital. The police started asking questions but everyone told them they hadn't seen shit. After the chaos had died down, Dub, D-Money, and Bobi shut the spot down and went to the hospital.

Dub called Slime's mother and told her what happened and told her to meet him at the hospital.

When he ended the call with her, he called Short Dogg and told him what happened and what hospital they were at, and Short let him know he was on his way. Short Dogg, Zell, and Danielle were eating steaks at a steakhouse in Addison. He asked the waitress to pack their remaining food in to-go trays, paid the tab, and immediately went to the hospital emergency room.

He called Big Dre and related the same information and Big Dre told him he would meet him at the hospital ASAP. When Short Dogg arrived to the hospital, he walked in the emergency room holding hands with Zell and Danielle. The parking lot was filled with niggas from Oak Cliff and the Lane, and everyone greeted him as he went inside.

He went straight to Slime's mother, and her two daughters were with her. "Hey, Mama Red," he said, hugging her.

Mama Red looked fifteen years younger than she was. She was tall and pretty with skin the color of toffee, and she had a huge ass. She had actually talked Short Dogg out of some dick years ago.

"Hey, Omar," she said, hugging him back.

"Mama, this is my wife Zell and our daughter Danielle."

"How are you doing?" Zell asked.

"I'm alright. Thank you for coming," she said. Then she looked to Short Dogg and asked, "How long have you been married?"

"Thirty-six days," they answered in unison.

"Oh. Congratulations," she told them.

"What's up, Bree and Toya?" Short Dogg asked Slime's two sisters. He used to fuck with Toya back in the day.

"Not much, Omar," Toya answered. Bree just shook her head and continued doing whatever she was doing on her phone.

Short Dogg knew Bree was still salty because he wouldn't fuck her when she'd tried to give him the pussy. What she didn't know was at the time she'd hit him up for some dick, he had literally just finished fucking her mama.

"What the doctors say about Slime?" he asked, Mama Red.

"He's in surgery right now. They hit my baby five times but the doctors won't know much else until he comes out of surgery. Do you know who did this to him?"

"Yeah, we know."

"What you plan on doing about it?"

"You from the same hood I'm from and you been knowin' me all my life, so you shouldn't even have to ask me a question like that," he said, looking her square in the eyes.

"I'm just askin' 'cause them niggas need to feel the same thing my son is feeling."

"When we get through with them niggas, they ain't never gonna feel nothin' else," Short Dogg said. As the words slipped through his lips, he could feel Zell squeeze his hand, as to let him know he was saying too much in front of way too many witnesses.

"Thank you, baby," Mama Red said. She hugged him again.

Not long after they finished talking, the doctor came out and told them that they had removed the bullets and that Slime was lucky no vital organs had been hit. He'd lost a lot of blood and they were going to keep him in the hospital for a week or two. The doctors explained that they would be watching him closely to ensure no infection set in. They also wanted to be sure the wounds healed properly. At the moment, he was sedated so they wouldn't be able to see him until morning.

Chapter 17

Just as the doctor was leaving, Big Dre walked in with three females. At the same time, Short Dogg's phone started vibrating. He looked at the screen and saw that the call was coming from the spot in the Estates.

"What up, Jojo?"

"Blood, them niggas just shot up the spot, but they didn't hit shit 'cause we saw the niggas coming."

"Y'all go 'head and shut the spot down and creep through the hood to see if you see them niggas."

"We on it," Jojo said, before ending the call.

"What up, Dre?" Short Dogg greeted.

"Zell told me lil bro gonna be ah'ight. Man, these the ladies I was tellin' you about," he pointed toward the three ladies. "I'm leavin' them with you 'cause I don't trust these niggas, blood. I don't trust nobody but them three niggas you grew up with— Dub, D-Money, and Bobi."

"Shalika called me and told me they killed Fred right before I got the call sayin' they shot Slime. I didn't wanna tell you that shit over the phone. She told me Kim was down with the plot to kill me," Short Dogg said, and shook his head, still in disbelief. Then Dub just told me that Slime said he saw Kim drivin' the car them niggas got out of when they shot him."

"That bitch foul. I knew it was somethin' about that pussy-eatin' bitch I didn't like. Them some dangerous, stupid lil niggas. We gotta end their days quick, fast, and in a hurry, before they end ours, my nigga. George was ready to lay them niggas down and he was tryna come put that work in tonight. Shit, I had to make the nigga chill 'cause his girl oldest daughter supposed to be graduating from Texas Southern University this weekend. He supposed to be going to H-Town but now he tryna cancel. I told him we got this shit and to go ahead and be there to see his daughter walk that stage."

"Man, George crazy."

"I gotta make a few runs but I'll get at you later," Dre said,

heading toward the exit.

"What's y'all's names," Short Dogg asked the girls after Dre left.

"I'm Em, this J-Low, and that's K-Rock," Em said, when she made the introductions.

"Well, I'm Short Dogg, this my wife Zell, and that's my daughter, Danielle," he said, and motioned Zell and Danielle over to introduce them. "Excuse me for a minute. Let me holla at my niggas then we can leave." He stepped away and left the ladies conversing with Zell and Danielle.

"Dub, y'all come here for a minute," he said, referring to Bobi and D-Money too. "Them niggas killed Fred earlier today at Shalika's spot, and a few minutes ago Jojo called and said they tried to shoot the spot up but they had seen them comin' so them niggas still ain't get shit."

"Jojo called us too. Man, how Fred let them niggas catch him slippin' like that?" D-Money asked.

"He went over there tryna talk some sense into them niggas and they smoked him," Dogg said, reiterating what he'd been told.

"Bro, I'm not gon' sleep 'til I bury one of them niggas for what they did to my lil nigga Slime and my nigga Fred," Dub said.

"Nah, y'all chill for now. I got a plan for them fools. I'll call y'all when I put everything together."

"Ah'ight, Dogg, get at us."

Short Dogg locked up with them and then headed back to where he'd left the ladies, to let them know it was time to go.

When they got inside his truck and pulled off, he turned on the music so nobody would ask any questions in front of Zell and Danielle.

When they got back to the house he took Em, K-Rock, and J-Low to his man cave and explained what was going on.

"First and foremost, we gotta get that bitch Kim," J-Low said.

"Yeah, you right," Em and K-Rock agreed.

"Let me call Shalika and see if she's heard anything yet." He pulled out a burner phone and called her. She answered on the first ring. "What's up?" he asked.

"Nothing yet. They ain't been back. Kim called to see if I was alright. I told her I was going to my mother's house for the night.

"Meet me in the parking lot of Kroger on Whitehurst and Skillman. I'll be there in about an hour," he said.

"Okay."

He left J-Low at the house with Zell and Danielle and took Em and K-Rock with him. He drove to Zell's old townhouse which was right down the street from the Kroger. He had Dub watching Shalika's apartment in case someone showed up or followed her. After they got settled in at the townhouse, he called Shalika and told her he was waiting on her.

Em was already parked in the parking lot. She looked around for anything suspicious as she waited for Shalika to pull up. She was going to take Shalika back to the house where Short Dogg and K-Rock were. He was on the phone with Em when Shalika called and told him she was in the parking lot.

"You see a black Chrysler 300 with a Black woman in it?"

"Yeah, she just pulled up beside me."

"Park your car and get in the car with her," Short Dogg instructed her, before ending the call.

When Shalika got to the townhouse, she rushed through the door. As soon as she saw Short Dogg, she ran into his arms and burst into tears again. "I can't get seeing all that blood out of my mind."

"Did they clean up the apartment?"

"Yeah, but that doesn't change the fact that he was killed in my living room right in front of me."

"Just chill for a little while longer and I'ma get you outta there," he said, still holding onto her, letting her get it out of her system. "I need your help."

"What you need me to do?"

"Listen to my lil sister, Em, and she gonna explain it to you."

Em took a small vial out of her bag and eyed Shalika as she walked over to her. She couldn't help but think to herself, damn, she's a bad bitch. Keeping her thoughts to herself, she said, "The next time he show up at your house, offer him a drink and try to put a couple of drops of this in it. It's odorless and has no taste," she said, handing her the vial of the clear liquid.

"What is this?" Shalika asked curiously. She stared at the vial as if she had never seen a clear liquid before.

"It's like a sleeping pill. You heard of the date-rape drug before, right?"

"Yeah."

"Well, that's it right there." Em nodded toward the vial.

"It's just gonna to put whoever drink it to sleep," Short Dogg said, taking her hand and pulling her to the back room. "When he goes to sleep, call me," he said, kissing her deeply, while squeezing her ass.

"Alright," she said, putting the vial in her pocket. "Can I suck that dick."

"Nah, I'm finna hit that pussy," he said, and proceeded to undress.

Short Dogg had no desire to cheat on Zell but duty called for it. He knew the safety of his life and his family's life depended on Shalika's help, so he had no choice but to lead her on. He laid her down on Danielle's old bed and pounded her back out.

Em was really mesmerized by Shalika's beauty and wanted to get to know her. She hadn't been that attracted to someone since she'd met J-Low and K-Rock.

She took Shalika back to her car and spent a little time asking questions and gathering information. She needed to speed up the process in eliminating the problem. She had already figured out that Kim was the brains behind Big Mack and Murda. Her training had taught her: if you cut off the head, the body would soon fall. So she got directions to Kim's house, the kind of car she drove, and her daily schedule.

When Shalika finally left, Em was surprised when she realized her panties were wet.

Chapter 18

When they got back to Short Dogg's house, Em explained what she'd learned from Shalika to J-Low and K-Rock. She grabbed her bag with her tools in it, went and found Danielle, and asked to borrow her car keys again.

Kim stayed in a three-story home in Cedar Hill. She'd had the home built for her and her girls. The home had six bedrooms, a four-car garage, two living rooms, seven bathrooms, four fireplaces, a swimming pool, and a spa. Five of her girls lived with her and all of them worked with her in one of her beauty salons.

When the alarm went off at 6:30 a.m., she got out of bed and walked through the house like a drill sergeant. "You bitches get up and let's get ready to make this money!"

The shop opened at 8:00 a.m. The girls had an hour to get ready before Kim hustled them out the door and over to the Suburban she drove to work every day.

As she took her shower, she thought back to all the events that had taken place in the past year, in her quest to become the queen of the streets of Dallas, Texas. Everything was falling into place like she wanted it to. All they had to do now was get rid of that nigga Short Dogg and her plan of being the crime boss of the M.O.B., the hardest clique the north had ever seen, would be finalized.

All along it had been her who had turned Big Mack and Lil Murda loose on all the nickel-and-dime hustlers who kept popping up in the hood.

Kim had even orchestrated the murder of Lil Charles and White Tammy by sending three of her girls in there to rob and kill them. She already had a plug. Mexican Rudy had connections to the cartel and he was ready to give her anything she needed. Big Mack didn't even know she had anything to do with the murders of Lil Charles and White Tammy. She had to get them out of the way. They were making too much money and had the weed game on lock.

When they started the M.O.B., she knew shit was falling into place. She had a whole team behind her. But when Short Dogg's brother blessed him with all that dope, her plan to flood the Lane with work from Mexican Rudy had been slowed down.

When Short Dogg gave her the dope for a little bit of nothing, she took it and flipped it. She felt like it was free money. She took her profit and started scoring from Rudy. Instead of shutting her spots down, she just moved them to different locations. She was moving work in Amarillo, Waco, Corsicana, and Oklahoma.

At first, Short Dogg was part of the plan, but he was being too difficult to control. She had to save Big Mack from the penitentiary because he was her muscle. That's why she came up with the plan to get a few witnesses to testify on the nigga who killed Kels, to free her little brother. Short Dogg was against that so he had to go.

When she got out of the shower she called Big Mack.

"What's up?" he answered.

"Y'all ain't murked that nigga yet?"

"That nigga got them Oak Cliff niggas all over this bitch. They been riding around all night looking for us," Big Mack said.

"Y'all be careful. But, we need to get rid of that nigga like yesterday," Kim said.

Big Mack could hear the urgency in her tone. "We on it as soon as we spot the nigga. Him and everybody with him."

"I'm about to head to the shop, but call me if something happen."

"Ah'ight," he said. He hung up and went back to sleep.

Kim put on her clothes and shoes and headed to the front door. "Come on y'all let's hit the road," she called out.

The ladies went out the door and got inside the truck. Y'all wake y'all asses up," Kim said as she put the key in the ignition and turned it.

BOOM!

The explosion lifted the truck twenty feet in the air, turning it into a big ball of flame and twisted metal. It blew the windows out of several of the houses close to Kim's. They never knew what hit them and nobody survived.

Down the street a safe distance away, Em watched the explosion. "Boom, bitches!" she yelled. As if nothing had happened, she put the car in drive and pulled off. When she made it back to the house, Short Dogg was sitting on the porch smoking a blunt.

"What's up, Em? You up early."

"I never went to sleep," she said, tossing him the keys. "Go watch the news ... your girl Kim had an accident," she told him, before going inside and closing the door behind her.

Chapter 19

When Big Mack found out that his sister was dead, first, he drove out to her house so he could see the damage with his own eyes. He saw the crime scene tape and there were investigators all over the place. He sat at the end of the street for over an hour, just watching all of the activity. When they loaded what was left of Kim's Suburban on the back of a flatbed truck to take it to the crime lab, he became so distraught, he called the last two people he trusted on earth.

"Lil Murda, blood, Kim gone."

"Where she went to, my nigga?"

"She dead, bro."

"What the fuck you talkin' about, blood? That nigga touched fam?" Lil Murda asked, getting crunk.

"I don't know what the fuck happened. All I know is the Suburban exploded in the front yard and killed everybody in the truck," Big Mack said. His voice started to break.

"Damn, that's fucked up. But, blood, that nigga ain't connected like that. Maybe the truck was just fucked up and exploded or caught on fire or something."

"Nah, Dogg, that's what I thought at first, but Kim's girl, Ebony, was at the house when the shit went down. That's who called me and told me what happened. She said the laws' preliminary investigation determined that it was an explosive device in the car."

"That gotta be something else. That nigga don't know shit about no bombs."

"Yeah, I feel that. I'ma find out what happened, and when I do, I'ma murk everybody in that nigga family," Big Mack said.

"We gon' do this shit together, fam," Lil Murda said.

"I'ma go chill with my baby mama for a lil bit, so I'ma get at you later, my nigga."

"Ah'ight, blood, one." Murda said, knowing his homie was grieving.

"One," Mack said. He ended the call and dialed his baby's mama.

"Hello," Gwen said when she answered the phone.

"What you doin'?"

Being a mother and a father 'cause yo' sorry ass ain't gonna do your part.

"Don't start that shit right now, Gwen. Somebody put a bomb in Kim's truck and killed her and four of her girls. I'm fucked up right now, and I just wanna come home and relax.

"Boy, stop playing like that."

"Nah, I'm for real. My big sister gone. It's all on the news."

"I'm sorry, baby."

"You want something to eat?" I'ma stop at Michele's and get me some Oxtails. You want somethin'?"

"Naw, baby, just come home."

"Ah'ight, I'll see you in a few."

"Hello," Shalika answered. At the moment, she was trying to calm herself after seeing Lil Murda's name on her phone screen.

"What's up, baby girl? You heard the news?"

"Her heart started racing when she automatically assumed something had happened to Short Dogg. She already knew how treacherous they were. She had witnessed that first hand. She forced herself to calm down before responding. Nah, what happened?"

"Somebody put a bomb in Kim's truck and the shit exploded with her, Erica, Kisha, Tay Tay, and Monica in it. They all dead."

"Boy, stop playin' on the phone. I just talked to Kim last night and she was home."

"It just happened early this morning. Ebony the only one left. She was sleep and wasn't in the truck. I just got off the phone with Mack and he fucked up. It's all over the news. I wouldn't even play like that."

"Damn, that's fucked up. The laws don't know shit?"

"Don't nobody know shit right now. Can I come over and chill with you for a minute?"

"I guess so since you going through some shit right now. But I'm still mad at you for that shit you and Big Mack pulled."

"We'll talk about that when I get there."

"Yeah, alright. I'll be here," she said and disconnected the call. She thought about calling Short Dogg but decided to wait until she put the fool to sleep.

***

Meanwhile, Short Dogg and Zell were planning their honeymoon. They had postponed it due to the weather. The forecast was clear now, so they had plans to charter a ship and make their honeymoon a family and friend outing.

They were going to invite twenty five to thirty people to go with them on a cruise to the Virgin Islands. They would board in Miami and spend two weeks on the cruise.

"Baby, we don't have to charter a ship we can just make reservations with one of the cruise lines. We can also reserve one of the ballrooms on the ship. It's a lot cheaper that way," Zell explained to him, as she looked online on her laptop.

"Whatever you decide to do, I'm with it. I just need a vacation somewhere in the sun where I can relax."

"Baby, you know you are not gonna relax. You're gonna wanna have sex all day and night."

"That be you. You can't control yourself when I come around you," he said playfully.

"Okay, if you say so. Let's make a bet. Let's see who can go the longest without sex until the cruise."

"That's a bet. I already know I'ma win. So what we gonna bet? We just can't make no bet without a wager."

"You make it light on yourself, tough guy," Zell said confidently.

"A hundred bucks to the winner," Short Dogg said. "Bet?" "Bet." She agreed.

Just as they finished making the bet, his cell phone rang. He looked at the caller ID and saw that it was Shalika calling. "What's up?"

"He sleep."

"Ah'ight," he said. He jumped up and grabbed his keys.

"Can you hurry before—

He interrupted her last thought for fear she would say too much over the phone. "I'm on it." He hung up and called Dub as he moved about hurriedly. "That fool at Shalika's apartment knocked out. Y'all go get him and meet me at the ranch." The ranch was a pig farm in Desota, a suburb of Dallas.

"On it right now. We already in the apartments. See you in a few," Dub quickly ended the call.

Short Dogg ran down the stairs and found the girls playing the Xbox with Danielle.

"Game time. He at Shalika house knocked the fuck out."

"Well, Danielle, your dad just saved you from a beatdown," J-Low told her.

"I'll be here to finish kicking y'all butt when you get back."

"Let's go put this nigga to sleep," Em said, when they got outside.

"Nah, Em, I gotta handle this nigga."

"Ah'ight, let's do it."

***

When they got to the ranch they went to the old slaughter house where the pigs where killed and butchered. Lil Murda had been laid out on the floor, tied up.

"That nigga woke?" Short Dogg asked.

"Yeah, his bitch ass woke," Dub said, kicking the shit out of the nigga. "Wake up fuck boy."

"Shalika said the nigga told her that Big Mack at his baby mama, Gwen house off Skillman in the Lofts. You want us to go get that nigga too?" Bobi asked.

"Nah, we gon' let the nigga see how it feel out here without his nigga," Short Dogg said. "But I got something for him," he added, coming up with an idea.

"'Sup, Lil Murda?" he said, as he squatted down and slapped the cowboy shit out of him with a nine millimeter.

"Fuck you nigga. Mack gon' blow yo' fuckin' brains out for this, nigga."

"Dumb ass nigga. Yo' big homie is a snitch. I'll never let the laws out think me," Short Dogg said. He slapped him with the gun again.

"You might as well kill me, nigga. 'Cause if you let me live, I'ma smoke er'thang you love."

"Okay. Oh, and tell Kim I said hi and bye."

"I know you ain't touch fam," Murda responded as if the thought alone pained him.

"Hell nah, I didn't, but she did," he said pointing at Em.

"Boom, bitches!" Em said smiling deviously.

"Bitch, I'ma kill you and yo' kids!"

"You ain't gon' kill nothin', fuck boy," Short Dogg told him, before shooting him three times in the head.

He went into one of the rooms and got a long, heavy, sword-looking knife, and chopped off Lil Murda's head with one swipe.

"Damn, blood, you trippin'," Dub said.

"I'ma send the nigga head to Big Mack's snitchin' ass. You said he at Gwen house over in the Lofts, right?"

"Yeah."

"Ah'ight, let's take this nigga out there to them pigs. Somebody grab his legs."

After they were back in the car and on the freeway, Short Dogg asked Em if she knew how to pick a lock?"

"Yeah, what's up?"

"I wanna put this fuck nigga head on another fuck nigga table while they sleep so it'll be the first thing that nigga see when he wake up."

"Let's do this shit," Em said, down for whatever. On the cool, she had a mini orgasm watching him chop the nigga's head off.

They headed for the Lofts.

Chapter 20

The next morning, Big Mack's four year old son woke up and climbed out of bed. He went to his parents' bedroom door and saw them still asleep in bed. He headed to the living room to turn the TV on so he could watch cartoons.

He saw uncle Murda's head sitting on the coffee table and thought it was a toy. He grabbed it and started playing with it. He rolled it across the floor and laughed when it stopped rolling.

The head was still leaking blood so Lil Johnny was covered in blood, and blood was all over the couch and floor.

His laughing woke Gwen up. She looked over and saw that Mack was still asleep and got up to see who he was playing with.

When she walked in the living room she saw what looked like blood all over Lil Johnny, as well as the floor and couch. He was holding something in his hands but she couldn't tell what it was. She walked closer to see what it was and screamed.

"Ahhhhhhhhhhhhhhhhhhh!" She let out the most terrifying scream and her body trembled with fear.

Big Mack heard her scream and was instantly awakened. He hopped out of bed, grabbed his pistol, and ran into the living room. Gwen was still screaming as she pointed at the head in Lil Johnny's hands.

"Noooo!" he yelled, running over and knocking the head

out of his son's hands. "Pack whatever you wanna take with you. We gettin' the fuck outta here. Hurry up!" he ordered Gwen. He picked his son up and rushed to the bathroom to wash the dead man's blood off of him.

He put Lil Murda's head in a trash bag and they carried everything out to his truck. He threw the head in the trash dumpster and took I-45 south and didn't stop until they were in Houston.

***

The next night, Short Dogg lay in bad after spending all day helping Zell make reservations and put the finishing touches on their vacation slash honeymoon.

Zell walked out of the bathroom in a Victoria Secret see-through négligée. She sat down on the bed and faced Short Dogg with her legs wide-open and started painting her toe nails.

Damn, baby got a fat ass pussy. I can see that clit pokin' out too. His dick was harder than steel.

She noticed him staring but acted like she didn't see him. Then, she got up and walked over to the dresser and bent over as if she were looking for another color of nail polish, giving him a rearview of her ass and pussy. She knew he loved looking at her ass.

Short Dogg was in a zone he'd unconsciously started caressing his dick. He let out a soft moan. Zell stood up and stomped her foot as if she were mad she couldn't find the right color of polish. Her ass jiggled.

He watched as her ass jiggle like Jell-O. He let out another moan, jumped up, and ran to the bathroom. "I'ma go take a shower," he said, over his shoulder.

"Okay, baby," she answered innocently.

As soon as the bathroom door closed, she burst out laughing because she knew she would soon be a hundred dollars richer.

A few minutes later Short Dogg walked out of the bathroom butt-naked with his dick poking out like a flag pole.

"Baby, can you put some lotion on my back?" he asked, with his dick mere inches from her face.

She paused painting her toenails, looked up, and let out a startled yelp which caused her to waste nail polish all over the bed.

"Shit, you scared me," she said. She attempted to clean up her mess but couldn't take her eyes off his dick.

He walked over to throw his wet towel in the dirty clothes hamper. When he turned around, she had two of her fingers on one hand stuffed in her pussy, while massaging her clit with two fingers on the other hand.

"Fuck that shit." He conceded. He picked up the pants he'd been wearing, dug in the pocket, pulled out a hundred dollar bill, and threw it to her. Then he buried his face between her legs.

***

George was just pulling back into the hotel parking lot when he saw Big Mack, Gwen, and Little Johnny checking in. He waited in the car until they got their key and went into their room. He called Polo, another one of their friends from Houston, they had been locked up with.

"Polo, man, I'm in the H. I need some heat with a silencer ASAP."

"I'm in the Ward, pull up."

Waiting, George sat in the parking lot for hours until he saw Big Mack walk out and get in the car. He followed him to McDonalds and watched him as he went inside and ordered. When he came back out, George was standing on the side of his car, in the dark, with his hoody over his face.

"Time's up, blood," he said, before emptying the clip in Big Mack's face.

Epilogue

Zell locked the door to her classroom. She walked outside and got in her car to drive to her old townhouse. Omar had explained everything that had taken place. He'd asked her if Shalika could live there and she'd agreed. Zell knew exactly who Shalika was and she knew that Shalika was in love with her husband. She'd met her at Lil Chris' funeral, saw her at his wake, and the little get-together they had after the funeral. She observed the way Shalika's eyes followed him everywhere he went as well her body language when she was close to him.

She was a woman, so she knew how women acted when they were in love, and she knew without a shadow of doubt Shalika was in love with *her* man. They needed to talk.

She parked, got out, and knocked on the door. A few minutes later, Shalika opened the door wearing shorts and a T-shirt.

"Hello," Zell said.

"Hi."

"Can I come in for a minute?"

"Sure, you're Short Dogg's wife, right?"

"Yes, I'm Zell," she said, sticking out her hand.

"I'm Shalika. Cone in and have a seat. Would you like something to drink?"

"No, I'm fine." She studied Shalika. *She's very pretty and her body is intimidating.*

Shalika was thinking the same thing about her. *Damn, this white girl is pretty and she got some ass.*

"Are you fuckin' my husband?"

Shalika was stunned. She started to say something fly but told herself Zell was too calm and respectful to be on some trip shit. So, instead, she replied, "Not since you got in my business and married him." She lied.

Zell laughed a little. She looked in her eyes as she talked, and for some strange reason, she believed her.

I know you're in love with him just like I am. Will you at least admit that?"

"I am." She responded truthfully.

"I think he likes you a lot too. I'm not sure if he's in love with you but I know he likes you. I watched the two of you at Chris' funeral and wake."

"I hope he does but I would never try and come between your relationship with him. He is really in love with you."

"I hope so too but why do you think that?"

"Because he married you and he's not the kind of man to marry or play with anyone. Every bit— I mean, every woman in the hood woulda dropped her panties for him if he wanted her to. But only one or two ever got him. You got a ring from him so I know he's madly in love with you. Plus, you beautiful and you got a nice body."

"Thank you. Are you really in love with him?"

"With every fiber of my body."

"Okay. I want you to move in with us. I love him that much too. And I want him to be completely happy. I grew up in a Mormon church."

Shalika was shocked. "Have you talked to him about this?"

"No, I haven't, but trust me, it'll be alright."

"So you willin' to share him with me?"

"Yes, as long as you can respect me as his wife and queen. I'm willin' to let you be our princess."

"I will always respect you and play my position. Thank you so much," Shalika said, with tears forming in her eyes. She ran over and hugged Zell.

"I'm having a baby! So you gonna be a god mother. Now go pack so we can get home, and I can tell him he's about to be a daddy."

"I'm so happy for you. Thank you so much, Zell."

When they made it to the house, Short Dogg hadn't made it in yet. Zell introduced Shalika to Danielle and told her that she was moving in with them. They cooked and ate then they went to the bedroom to shower and put on négligées and wait on Omar to come home.

When he got home later that night, he had picked up a carryout meal from Michele's Soulfood. He had Oxtails, cabbage, sweet potatoes, and hot water cornbread. When he walked in the bedroom and saw Zell and Shalika both sitting in the bed in négligées, painting each other's toenails, he dropped his bag on the floor in surprise.

"Oh shit!"

"Hey, baby," Zell said, looking up briefly before continuing to paint Shalika's nails.

"Hi, Short Dogg," Shalika said.

"Hi. What are y'all doing in here?"

"Waiting on you," Zell answered.

"Listen, Zell, can I talk to you outside for a minute."

"Sure, honey," she answered sweetly to him, and whispered to Shalika, "we'll be right back."

They walked outside and sat on the porch. "How did she get here?"

"I went and got her from the townhouse. She's in love with you just as I am, and her loyalty should be rewarded. What she did for us with the Lil Murda situation coulda saved your life. I knew she was in love with you the first time I saw her at Chris' funeral. She couldn't take her eyes off you and I think you like her too. I grew up in the Morman church, so it's alright. She told me you stopped seeing her before we were married. And as long as she respects that I'm the queen and she's the princess, we'll be good."

"I didn't know you were into women."

I only did that once with my roommate in college but I'm into anything that makes you happy, baby."

"You make me happy."

"Together, we'll make you happier, besides she's beautiful and her body is incredible. Are you scared? What? You can't handle two bad chicks at the same time?"

"I ain't never scared!"

"Show me and come fuck the shit outta both of us," she said, hugging and kissing him. And, oh yeah, I almost forgot...You gonna be a father. I'm pregnant."

"Stop playin', baby. For real?" he asked, excitedly.

"For real."

"Oh shit! Thank you, thank you, thank you. That's my son in there," he said, rubbing her stomach.

"No, that's *our* daughter."

"How you know? Did they already tell you that it's a girl?"

"Not yet, but I already know."

"Well, it's a boy. But either way, I don't even care as long as he or she is healthy, I'll be happy with one or the other. I'm naming her okay?"

"Maybe. Come fuck the shit outta both of us and you can name her."

"You ain't said shit. Let's go," he said, slapping her on the ass.

One month later...

They rented two huge RVs and hired two drivers to drive them to Galveston so they could board the ship for their cruise. They had decided that the women would ride in one RV and the men would ride in the other.

Pops, Junior, B-Dub, Short Dogg, Glenn, Jay, George, and Big Dre would be in the men's RV. And riding with the females would be Faye, Connie, Zell, Shalika, Kawanna, J-low, K-rock, and Em.

They had loaded the RVs at Short Dogg's house at 5:00 a.m. and set off for Galveston. As soon as they drove off, Junior started asking questions about Zell and Shalika.

"Bro, how you pull that off? You got two of the baddest chicks in the Triple D and they know about each other. That's some real pimp shit right there. Zell is bad with a capital 'B', but Shalika is video vixen."

"It wasn't even me. Zell did that on her own," Short Dogg answered honestly.

"That boy got that shit right there from me. I taught that nigga that player shit," Pops said.

Mama gon' kick yo ass if she hear you talkin' that shit," Junior said. They laughed.

"Lil nigga, yo' mama know I'm a playa. When she met me I was a playa. That's how I pulled her."

"How you pull Mama Faye, Pops?" Glenn asked.

"Y'all really ain't gon' believe this, but I really didn't pull Faye... She pulled me. Check this out...

Twenty-year-old Derrick "Pops" Wilson had gotten his nickname from sucking on Blow Pops all the time. He was a stick up kid and he'd received a call from his source that an old White man who owned several fur coat factories around the city, had hundreds of thousands of dollars at home in a safe. He'd lucked up and got the address, the code to the safe, and the directions to where the safe was located.

Then Pete, his source, told him, "I wanna send somebody else on this one with you."

"You know I don't work like that, Pete."

"I know, but that's the only way you gon' get this job. This is a major lick and I already promised this one to another person. I'm cuttin' you in on their paper. So, if you want the job call this number and y'all work together."

"Who is this nigga?"

131

"They solid. I been fuckin' with them just as long as I been fuckin' with you."

"I'ma trust you on this one, but I work alone so no more two-man jobs."

"This gonna be the biggest lick you ever hit."

"Give me the number."

He gave him the information and told him to hit the lick on Friday. It was only Tuesday so Derrick had a few days to get his mind right for the job.

Pops hung up the phone and mumbled, *"Fuck that nigga. I got all the information I need now. I ain't fuckin' with no nigga I don't know, and I damn sho' ain't lettin' no nigga in on my play."* Pete might get mad but fuck it, he'll get over it when I drop that cash at his feet, he thought.

***

Friday night, Pops pulled up and parked down the street where he could watch the lick's house. It was dark and raining outside so he didn't worry that someone might be outside and notice his car. Plus, the car was stolen anyway. He had stopped by McDonalds and got two Big Macks, large fries, and a strawberry milkshake. He was eating and watching the house when the passenger door opened. A nigga dressed in all black jumped in and closed the door. Dark glasses covered his eyes and a black hoody draped his head.

"You gotta be Pops. I'm Faye, and don't no nigga get in on my lick and try to cut me out. Pete told me you was gonna pull some shit like this that's why I been out here watching the house since Tuesday."

Pops could tell it was a female but he couldn't see any of her features because of the hoody and the dark shades. *"I was gon' call you. I was just casing the place out."* Pops lied.

"Yeah, right. Anyway the house keeper left about a hour ago, so the house empty right now.

"How you know it's empty?"

"I looked through the windows."

"By now, Pops had finished eating, so he pulled out one of his blow pops and stuck it inside his mouth.

"I see you a inconsiderate nigga. You ain't gon' offer me one of those suckers?"

He reached in his pocket and gave her one but continued to watch the house. He was still heated that he had to hit the house with someone he didn't know.

They watched for another twenty minutes before he finally said, "You ready? Let's do this shit."

They got out of the car and made their way to the house. The house was a huge three-story home on the rich side of town. They slipped on their gloves and made their way to the side where a side window had been left unlocked by the house keeper.

Faye lifted the window and silently slipped inside. After Pops was inside, they stood for a moment and listened for any sounds that someone might've been inside. He saw Faye pull out a twenty-two with a silencer on it, and she motioned him to follow her. She walked from room to room making sure no one was home.

After they checked all three floors, she went directly to the master bedroom and lifted the carpet on the side of the bed. She dialed in the combination to the safe, and when it clicked open she saw bundles of money. "Bingo!" she said.

She pulled a bag out of her pocket and began to fill it with the money. At the bottom of the safe was a large jewelry box, and she took that too.

When the safe was emptied they walked back through the house and started collecting valuables. The took paintings, a few vases, and cleaned out a gun cabinet. They made their way back out the window, and to the car. Pops took one bag, and Faye took the other bag to her car, which was parked a little further down the street. They followed one another back to the motel room where they were supposed to meet Pete and split the money.

When they pulled up and parked, Pops grabbed the bag with the paintings and other stuff in it, but Faye stopped him.

"That's our shit. He don't get no parts of that." Pops didn't question her, instead, he simply put the items back in the car.

Then they walked up to the room door and knocked. When Pete let them inside, they counted him out one hundred thousand and left.

Once they were back in the parking lot, Faye looked at Pops and said, "Follow me so you can ditch that car, then we can go split that other loot and count the rest of this money."

"Let's roll," he said.

They ditched the car and Pops got in Faye's car with her. She drove to the Budget Suites where she had already rented a room. They went inside and counted the money which totaled three hundred and eighty thousand dollars. They walked away with one hundred and forty-thousand apiece, minus the hundred they paid Pete.

"I got a hookup who'll buy all that other shit. Let me call the nigga and get him over here." She made the call and an hour later they split another eighty thousand.

Pops made a call and got someone to pick him up. "I like the way you work. Maybe we'll do this again," he said, and they exchanged numbers.

Three weeks later...

They sat in the car watching the traffic at a trap. Faye got a call on her cell phone and listened for a second. "On the way," she said, then turned to Pops. "Let's roll. They countin' the bread right now, and the backdoor is unlocked. There's three niggas inside. My source got on the red Gucci shirt."

Faye reached underneath the seat and pulled out a 9 mm with a silencer attached and an extended clip.

"What you got?" she asked Pops.

He pulled out a .40.

"Here use this," she said, pulling out another 9 with an extended clip and silencer attached.

They walked to the back of the house and went in the backdoor. Once inside, they stood in the kitchen. They could here loud music and the sound of a money counter clicking. Faye looked back and motioned Pops to follow her. Of course, Pops was sucking on a blow pop.

"Alright, you niggas reach for the sky!" she said, stepping in the room. She saw piles of money, drugs, and the money counter sitting on a table. One of niggas reached for the chopper that was lying on the table, but Faye shot him point-blank range in the chest.

"Ugh," the nigga said, as he fell to the floor clutching his chest.

"I hate repeating myself," she said, and ran over and kicked the nigga in the face.

Damn, this bitch straight gangsta, Pops thought. He pulled the bag out and put the drugs, the money, the money counter, and the chopper in it. Faye searched the niggas and took their guns, money, and jewelry. She tied the niggas up and left the ropes on her source a little looser so he could free himself after they left. Then they left as quietly as they came.

Faye started the car and drove in the direction of the Budget Suites, but Pops stopped her and said, "Fuck that Budget Suites shit. Go to this spot." He gave her the directions and twenty minutes later they pulled up to a nice brick home in Ellum Thicket.

"Come on in," he said, as he opened the car door and got out. He grabbed the bag and headed to the front door. He unlocked the door and they went inside to an expensively-furnished home.

"Who shit this is?" Faye asked.

"What you mean, who shit is this? This my shit," Pops *told her. He led her to the den and told her to make herself comfortable. "Let me go check on my boys," he said, and left the room.*

When he came back she had took her hoody off her head and removed her shades. He was stunned when he saw her. She had long, black hair, a honey colored complexion, and light-brown eyes. She was Halle Berry pretty. He couldn't see her body because she had on baggy clothing, but he could tell she wasn't skinny.

He pulled out the money counter and together they counted the money.

"You got kids?" she asked.

"Yeah, I got three boys."

"Where they mama at?" She questioned him further.

"Damn, you nosey," he said smiling.

She looked at him and thought... this nigga is really nice looking. Pops was about six foot four, slim, and high-yellow with good hair.

"One dead and the other locked up," he said, after a long pause.

"I got two," she said.

"You got two kids?"

"A girl and a boy."

"Where they daddy at?" he asked, sticking a sucker in his mouth.

"Damn, you nosey." They chuckled. "He died in a car accident."

"Oh, sorry to hear that," he said.

"I'm good," she replied.

"You want something to drink?" he asked her. He got up and walked over to the bar to fix himself a Crown and coke.

"Yeah, let me get one of them. You got some smoke?"

"Yeah, I keeps me some weed. Hold on."

He left and came back with a bag of Kush and some cigars. They smoked, drinked, and talked until she fell asleep on the couch. When she woke up the next morning, she heard the sound of children giggling. When she'd opened her eyes three little boys were standing over her, staring.

"Hey, how are you little guys doing?"

"We alright," the oldest one answered.

"What's y'all's names?"

"I'm Glenn," the oldest one answered again.

"I'm Jay."

"I'm Dell."

"What's your name?" the smallest one, Dell, asked.

"My name is Faye."

"Are you my daddy girlfriend?" he asked curiously.

"No, we just work together."

"I'm hungry. Can you cook us something to eat."

"Your daddy still sleep?"

They nodded.

"Show me where the bathroom is. Let me wash up and then I'll cook you something to eat, okay?"

"Yes, ma'am." Dell took her hand and showed her to the bathroom.

She went in and opened the medicine cabinet and some drawers. She found a new toothbrush and a face towel. She brushed her teeth and washed her face, used the toilet and washed her hands again.

When she opened the bathroom door, Dell was waiting in the hallway for her. "Come on, Ms. Faye. I'ma show you where everything at so you can cook."

Faye scrambled eggs, fried bacon, made grits and biscuits, and poured each of the boys a glass of orange juice. They sat down at the table to eat and she joined them. It felt so natural to her, and the boys too

While they were eating, Pops entered the kitchen. "Did they make you cook them something to eat?"

"No, I just did it," she lied and winked at them.

"I sent the babysitter home last night after you fell asleep on me. I put your money up too. I'll get it for you. Any of that food left?" he asked, while pointing at their plates.

"Yeah, we left you some."

"I don't wash dishes," Faye said, after they finished eating and cleared the table.

"I got that," Pops said. He put the dishes in the dishwasher. The count on the money was two hundred ninety thousand," he informed her. "We gon' give the source fifty stacks and that'll leave us one twenty a piece. It's all counted out and banded up," he added. He sat the bag on the table.

Faye got her half and the fifty for the source and told Pops she'd would call him later. She went in the den where the boys were playing video games. "It was nice meeting you guys. I'll see you later."

"Thank you, for cooking for us, Ms. Faye," the boys said, one after another.

They some nice, well-mannered little boys, she thought, as she made her way home.

Two weeks later…

They sat in Pete's office and listened as he gave them the details on some info he'd gotten about a diamond dealer. The dealer was in Dallas for a convention, with millions of dollars' worth of rare diamonds.

"This could be the lick we need to retire. If y'all can pull this off successfully, I'm definitely retiring. We could all walk away millionaires," he explained.

He showed them a picture of the diamond dealer, a middle-aged White man. He told them what hotel he was staying in and the room number. The convention was scheduled for Friday and Saturday.

Pops brought his boys over to Faye's house. Her best friend, Kay Kay, was staying with her, and she would be watching the kids while they handled their business.

"Hey, Ms. Faye," the boys said, as they walked in the door.

"How y'all doing?" she asked, as Dell ran over to her and gave her a hug.

"We alright."

"Come on and let me introduce y'all to my babies." She took them in the den where Connie and Omar were watching a movie. "This is my daughter, Connie. And that's my son, Omar. This is Glenn, Jay, and Dell. Y'all be good while we gone and don't give Ms Kay Kay no trouble."

"We won't," Dell said. He sat down next to Connie and Omar. Pops was just standing there looking on. "So you ain't gon' introduce me to yo/ kids?"

"Oh, I forgot about you. Connie, Omar, y'all come here. This is Mr Pops. This is Connie and Omar."

"How y'all doing?"

"Alright."

"Who's the oldest?" he asked.

"I am. I'm five and Omar is four."

"You the same age as Dell," he told her.

He was talking to the kids but he couldn't keep his eyes off Faye's ass and hips. She was wearing jeans that fit her like a glove. He was in a zone. This girl is bad.

As they were leaving, she turned and caught him staring at her ass. Quit gawkin' like that 'cause it make you look like a predator."

"Girl, ain't nobody lookin' at you."

"Yeah, right."

They got in Faye's car and drove to the Budget Suites. She went to the room that she rented by the week. She changed into her all-black clothes and hoody. While there, she grabbed her .22 with the silencer. Then they drove to the W Hotel and parked where they could watch the Lincoln the White man had rented.

After about an hour, they saw him exit the building and get into the car. They followed him to the Market Center where they were having the convention.

"He got about four hours before he come back out," Pops said, pulling out a blow pop and putting it in his mouth.

"Why you always suckin' on them lollipops, nigga? You ever tried suckin' on some pussy?"

"Nah, I don't eat pussy 'cause that's nasty."

"How eatin' pussy nasty, lame ass nigga? You came outta a pussy. If it wasn't for pussy yo' red ass wouldn't be here."

"All that's fine and dandy but I don't eat pussy."

"You like gettin' yo' dick sucked, don't you."

"Hell yeah! I don't know a nigga that don't like head."

"You want a bitch to suck your dick but you don't eat pussy? You crazy. How that add up? Have you ever even tried to suck a pussy?"

"Nah, I aint never tried it."

"Well, how you know you don't like it if you ain't never tried it?"

"I don't want no funky ass pussy smell all on my face."

"What kind of bitches you been fuckin' with if they pussy stink?"

It was dark outside and they were in a huge parking lot. Faye undid the drawstring on her sweat pants and pulled them down. She pulled her thong to the side and said, "Smell this pussy and tell me what it smell like."

Pops looked over and saw her shaved pussy. The lips on her pussy were so fat, and so much darker than her skin, it looked like she had a hamburger between her legs.

"Smell it, nigga."

He leaned down and inhaled her aroma.

"What it smell like?" *she asked, letting him see her massaging her clit.*

"It smells like coconut."

"So, do it stink?"

"Nah," he answered. His gaze was on her fingers as she rubbed on her button.

"Smell it again."

This time when he leaned down to smell her, she grabbed the back of his head and pulled his face in to her pussy. She opened her pussy lips with two fingers to show him her clit. Lick that right there." For a long time he just inhaled her scent. Then she finally felt his warm tongue. "What it taste like?" she asked breathless.

He didn't even bother to answer. He just kept licking.

"Suck on it a little. Oh shit, yeah, just like that. Lick it faster. Now suck it a little bit. Damn, I'm 'bout to nut. Oh shit, I'm nuttin'... suck on it now. Alright, stop. I'm through," she said, and pushed his head away.

"Now was it nasty, nigga?"

"Nah, that shit tasted good. Why you make me stop? Let me finish."

"You did finish. I nutted already. All them damn lollipops made you a beast. You got some fire ass head."

"Fuck with me on some head now."

"Boy, you crazy!"

"What you me—

"Here come that White man. Get yo' head off yo dick and get back in game mode. If you play your cards right you might get more than some head," she told him. She pulled her clothes up and got ready to follow the mark.

They followed him back to the hotel to wait for an opportunity to hit the lick. The mark never stopped or gave them a chance to take him. They still had one day to hit him. The hotel had too much security so they didn't want to hit him at the hotel.

"We might have to hit him at a red light. Just pull up on the side of him and pop his ass then jump in the car with him and drive off," Pops said.

"That's a possibility but let's make that the last option."

Just as they finished discussing the possibility of having to shoot the White man, Pete called on Pop's phone.

"Hey, don't shoot that White man. Tomorrow, he's going to make a few stops, Just take the whole car, and the brief case with the diamonds in it will be in the car. Come by, I got a spare key to the car."

"We on the way right now." Pops hung up.

They arrived at Pete's and he gave them a car key to the car along with the pad that locked and unlocked the car doors.

"Y'all need to go get some disguises and a car that can't be traced back to you. They got cameras in gas stations. Even if the police don't put much time into investigating a theft, the insurance company damn sure will. So make sure y'all don't leave nothing to lead them back to us. We gonna split two million between us. We gotta give the White man a million. I already got a buyer so y'all just get the diamonds and get them to me."

Pete and Faye left and headed to the mall where they bought wigs, fake mustaches, and beards to disguise themselves with. They want back to Faye's house. Since they knew they ware going to be busy the following day, Pops stayed there for the night. Besides, that way, he would have someone to watch his boys while he and Faye handled business...

"So, that's how I met Faye y'all," Pops said when he finally concluded his recollection.

"Pops, you do realize Mama Faye straight played you outta your dome?" Glenn told him.

"Yeah, we still laugh about that shit right to this day."

"What happened to you suckin' on the lolipops?" Omar asked.

"Yo' mama broke me up from that shit. She said if I was gonna be her man I couldn't be suckin' on suckers all day and night."

"Mama Faye a straight made 'G'," Dell said.

"Did y'all hit the lick on the White man for the diamonds?" Jay asked.

"Yeah, we got him the next day," Pops said, firing up a blunt.

"I'm finna take a nap, but wake me up when we get close," Pops said, after they finished the blunt. He closed his eyes and reminisced about the part of the story he couldn't tell them...

After they got back to Faye's house, they made a pallet for the kids and turned on a movie for them to watch in the den. They sat at the kitchen table and smoked a few blunts and had some drinks.

"I can't believe I let you play me outta my head like that," Pops told her.

"Nigga, you wanted to eat this pussy so stop playing."

"Nah, that ain't true. That was the first time I ever got down like that, for real."

"If that was your first time, I'd hate to see you with a little practice. You got a nice head on your shoulders," she said smiling.

"I guess you think I should be flattered?"

"Hell yeah. You should be flattered you even got to taste this pussy, nigga. I ain't had no kind of sex since my kid's daddy died two years ago."

Pops went to the spare bedroom, showered, and got in the bed. He went to sleep thinking about fucking the shit out of Faye's fine, red ass.

Sometime, during the middle of the night, he woke up to Faye giving him the best blow job he'd ever had in his life.

"Oh shit, Faye. Put that pussy in my face... I wanna taste you again."

"You ain't said shit, nigga," she said, and climbed on top of him in the sixty-nine position. She started sucking and

slurping on his dick, and at the same time, he was sucking and slurping on her pussy.

I'm finna cum all over your face! Damn, I'm cummin'," *she said, grinding on his face.*

"I'm about to bust too." She started deep throating his dick while masssging his nuts, until she felt him unload in her mouth.

"Damn, boy, how long it been since you nutted?" she asked him, after swallowing what seemed like a cup of cum.

"That shit been building up every since I saw you in them jeans."

"Your dick game better not be trash or I'ma clown yo' ass," she told him, as she turned around and sat on his dick.

"Damn, this pussy good," he said, once he was buried inside of her. "Oh shit, I'm finna nut."

"You better not, muthafucka. You finna fuck me!"

"I'm just playin'," he laughed. He grabbed her hips and pulled up into her.

"This .... ain't ... no ... time .... to ... be .... playin..."

He didn't even respond. He just grabbed her around the waist, flipped her over, and pounded her back out. They made love all night.

The next morning they woke up and did it again.

"You know you are my woman now, right?"

"Boy, you crazy. Just 'cause I gave you some pussy don't mean I'm your woman."

I feel you on that. But see, we too much alike. We compatible, and you might not even believe this, but I'm in love with you."

"That's lust, nigga, that ain't love."

"Nah, I know what lust is. I fell in love with you when we first started hittin' licks together. Seein' how square business you was about your money, that gangsta side of you, and just seein' how you interact with yo' kids and my kids. That shit right there did it for me."

Faye sat quietly, thinking about what he was saying. She loved kids and had already practically feel in love with his sons, especially Dell. She'd already noticed how starved they were for some sort of motherly love. Just the same, her kids needed a father figure in their life also. There was only so much a woman could do raising a son.

"Okay, say we do this, I ain't exceptin' no cheatin' ass nigga," she told him.

I ain't even that kinda nigga. I ain't had no pussy in damn near six months 'cause I'm not with that one-night-stand shit. If she ain't got wifey qualities, I'll pass. I don't need three or four different women to make me feel more like a man. I just want one pussy that's mine, that I can love on and make love to."

"You talk a good game. I hope this ain't no bullshit you spitting. So, do I have wifey qualities?"

"Yeah, I think you do."

"Let me ask you a question and I want you to be honest."

"I promise."

"You ate pussy before, didn't you?" She had to ask him that. She didn't believe he had never ate pussy. His head was too good for that to have been his first time.

He laughed before he said, "Nah, I already told you that. That was my first time."

"You know if you my man now, I'ma need some more of that," she said smiling.

"You got that every night."

Two months later they were married.

***

In the females bus, Faye entertained the girls with stories of her past. She told them about the lick they hit on the White man for the diamonds.

"The White man really robbed his own damn self. He set the whole play up for us to get the diamonds. He got a

145

million for the diamonds after we sold them. Then, he got the insurance money 'cause the diamonds were insured. So, he came away with like four million."

"How did y'all finally get the diamonds?" K-Rock asked.

"We dressed up like an old man and an old lady. When he parked at the gas station, Pops got in his car and we drove off. The diamonds were in the car in a briefcase. That was the easist six hundred thousand I ever made."

"Mama, what y'all do with all that money?" Connie asked.

"Girl, we been livin' off that money."

"So that was yall last lick?" Shalika asked.

"Yep, that was the last lick we pulled. We were lucky and we had kids to raise. We knew we had enough money to live off of the rest of our lives if we invested it right. So we decided to let it all go and go straight legal."

"Now, Shalika, tell me about every thing that been goin' on with you," Fays said.

Shalika looked at Zell nervously. Well, Mama Faye I just been working and—

"Shalika, tell me what happened at your house with Fred."

"They were talkin' about killin' Omar and Fred told them that if they went at him they would have to get him too. So, they shot him right in my living room."

"And Kim triflin' ass was down with the shit too?" Faye asked.

"She was the ring leader."

"That bitch used to call me mama and eat at my table. That just goes to show that you don't know what nobody is thinking or who to trust. I wish I could get my hands on that bitch. She'd make me forget I changed my life."

"You ain't gotta worry about her ever again," Em told her. "Her truck went BOOM," she added smiling.

"Yeah, I seen that shit on the news. So Big Mack still out there somewhere plottin'?"

"Nah, Mama Faye.," Kawanna told her, "he got shot down in Houston at a hotel."

"In Houston? How you know that?"

"Me and George were in Houston for my daughter's graduation from TSU and we were at the Hotel. They found him at the ice machine shot dead. George recognized him."

All the women were surprised by the information because they thought he was still out there waiting to make his move.

"Do Omar know that?" Faye asked.

"I'm pretty sure George done told him by now."

"I wonder what he got hisself into?" Faye asked, looking intensely at Kawanna.

Discreetly, Zell picked up her cell phone and called Omar. "Baby, did you know Big Mack was killed in Houston at a hotel?"

"How you find that out?"

"Kawanna just told us that her and George was at the hotel when they found his body."

"George ain't said nothin' to me about it. Let me go holla at him and I'ma get back at you. How y'all doing over there?"

"We okay. Your mama was tellin' us about how she met Pops."

"You feelin' okay?"

"I'm fine, stop worrying."

"You don't think you gonna get seasick or nothin' like that bein' that you pregnant?" "

"No, I'll be alright. Stop worrying. I'm only eight weeks, baby."

"Ah'ight, give my love to my princess. I love you, baby."

"Love you too."

Short Dogg hung up the phone and went back over and took a seat next to George and Big Dre. The two were deep in conversation. "You got somethin' to tell me, my nigga?" he asked George.

"Nah, why? What's up?" George asked, as if he really didn't know.

"Stop playin' games and tell me what happened in Houston."

"The graduation was beauty—

"What happened to Big Mack?"

"Oh, that. I don't know what happened but they found the nigga shot to death at the same hotel we were staying at."

"What a coincidence. I guess you didn't have nothin' to do with it either?"

"Hell nah, nigga. I was in my room all night with my wife."

"Hold up, wait," Big Dre said.

"So Big Mack got killed at the same motel you was stayin' at in H-Town and you didn't have shit to do with it?"

"*Hotel,* nigga, we don't do motels. And yeah, '*the nigga got smoked at the same hotel'* and I ain't have shit to do with shit. I told you niggas, I'm out the game."

"Bro, I know your sneaky ass. You can fool these niggas with that bullshit but I know you," Big Dre said.

"You trippin', fat ass nigga. I'm tellin' you, I was in my room all night. The nigga dead so the shit is over with. Short Dogg need to get back to the money and stop worrying about them fuck niggas. You need to weed out anybody that had any loyalty to them niggas and get rid of they ass too."

"I never trusted them lil niggas." Dre said.

"I'ma throw some shit in the air and see who catch it when we get back. Then I'ma smoke every nigga who think he wanna be loyal to that snitchin' ass nigga. The shit crazy, how niggas bite the hand that feed them. I never woulda thought Kim would turn out to be like that" Dub said, shaking his head.

"Me either," Short Dogg added.

"This shit woulda hurt Lil Chris. Kim was like a sister to all of us. If it wasn't for Shalika, a nigga probably never woulda knew Kim was foul 'til it was too late," Dub said.

"That's some real talk right there." Glenn said.

"The bitch was plottin' the whole time but I don't trust Shalika either," Big Dre said.

"Why you bringin' her up in this bullshit?" Short Dogg asked, getting heated.

"Bro, you my nigga and I know you got feelings for her. But, I'm just tryna look out for my nigga and it's been too much fuck shit goin' on with that whole little crowd. Her and Kim was tight. I can't believe she ain't know about this shit."

Pops woke up and heard the last statement Big Dre had made and saw the look on Omar's face and he knew he was getting heated.

"Omar, you didn't lace Dre up on what Shalika did?"

"I guess I didn't."

"Dre, Shalika set the nigga Murda up so Omar could get at him. If it wasn't for her, we would still be lookin' to get at the nigga. Plus, she the one who laced him up that Kim was even involved in the bullshit from jump. Nobody would have expected that Kim was involved in the shit. Shalika did that. So y'all lay off her," Pops said.

"Damn, I didn't know all that. Why you didn't tell me that part of the story, my nigga?" he asked Short Dogg.

All this shit happened so fast, I'm still kinda fucked up I didn't see this shit myself. In the last month, three muthafuckas I thought I would die for are dead. I was going to holla at you and George about all this shit once we got on the boat. All this shit is crazy."

"We can't change shit that already happened. Some niggas don't know what loyalty is. Ain't shit we gonna be able to tell Omar about Shalika until we have some solid proof that she foul. Personally, I trust her. Shit, she going down for murder too if the shit hit the fan. She put date rape drugs in the nigga drink and called Omar when the nigga passed out. So she just as guilty as everybody else."

Short Dogg sat back contemplating what Dre had said. He thought back on all that had taken place to see if he had missed anything. Shalika didn't have to tell him shit about Kim or that they had killed Fred. She didn't even have to set Murda up like she did. He already knew she was tight with Kim. But that was because Kim was either sucking her pussy or trying to suck her pussy. He had never asked about their relationship because he really didn't give a fuck.

He knew Shalika had feelings for him and he had feelings for her too. But he was in love with Zell, and he would have never perused a relationship with Shalika other than some occasional head or pussy from her. Zell felt like she wanted to bring her in, and he couldn't deny having two bad bitches to share his bed with him every night was a blessing.

He had given Shalika a hundred thousand dollars to put in her bank account. So, if she wanted to leave or if she didn't feel like shit was going the way she wanted it to, she could leave and have a little nest egg to fall back on. But he knew in his heart that she was solid and he didn't have to worry about fuck shit with her. He sat back and closed his eyes to take a little nap before they got to the ship.

Back on the female bus, K-Rock, Em, and J-Low sat talking quietly amongst themselves.

"Damn, Mama Faye fine as hell. I wanna suck her pussy," K-rock said.

"Girl, Short Dogg gonna kill you about his mama, but she is fine. I wanna have a orgy with Short Dogg and Shalika. I know that nigga got some good dick and some fire ass head too. He got them sexy ass lips too. If I get the chance while we on this ship, I'ma just ask the nigga for some of that dick," Em told them.

"I gotta have that White girl. Zell is so fine, the other night when I was doing her toes, her pussy so fat I could see the lips through her shorts. My pussy was so wet I had to go take a shower and get my vibrator out. I think she know I want her too. I can tell by the way she be looking at me with that little smirk on her face. She knows. I'm just like you, Em, if

I get the chance I'm just gon' ask her if I can eat her out just one time," J-Low admitted.

"We all about to get fired from the best job we have ever had 'cause you freaky ass bitches can't control yourselves," Em said laughing.

"You too bitch. I know you got the hots for Short Dogg. Bitch, you cant take your eyes off him, and anytime he wanna go somewhere you always volunteer to go with him," K-Rock said.

"I'm just doing my job by protecting our bossman."

"Yeah, right, bitch. You tryna get fucked with that big ass dick he got."

"How you know it's big? Did you see it?" Em asked getting excited.

"I saw the print, and unless the nigga had a Coke bottle in his pants, he working with a monster," K-Rock said, and they all burst out laughing.

"I like him. We can't let nothin' happen to that nigga," Em said.

"Yeah, me too. Everybody in the whole family cool. Especially Danielle. That's my little sister all over again," J-Low said.

"I'm down with all that. I like him too, but I'ma still shoot my shot at Mama Faye. I gotta have some of that pussy. Look at all that ass 'bout to bust out them pants," K-Rock said.

Faye being wise to all game, knew exactly what was going on in all of their minds. All you had to do was watch, listen, and pay attention, and alot of shit was obvious. She knew Em was very fond of Omar and Shalika by the way she stayed close to them. Any time they were all in a room together she always found some kind of way to be close to one of them.

She knew that J-Low was infatuated with Zell. She couldn't keep her eyes off Zell, and Faye had caught her several times looking at Zell's ass.

She knew K-Rock was feeling her. It was turning her on too knowing that she had this young girl feeling like that about her. Every time she looked up, she was staring at her. Faye thought to herself.... *this little young bitch is bold too 'cause she don't even look away when I catch her staring at me. The first chance I get I'ma see if she really 'bout it,* Faye told herself.

She had already been watching Shalika to see where her loyalties were, and she had came to the conclusion that she was one hundred percent in love with Omar.

When they finally stopped at a gas station, Faye was able to catch K-Rock alone and she went over to talk to her.

"Why you keep watchin' me, little girl?"

"I'm a grown woman, Ms. Faye, but I'm watchin' you 'cause I think you very beautiful, fine, and sexy."

Thank you. But, what does all that mean? I'm married and my husband is here with us."

"I know that."

"So you wanna have sex with me, don't you?"

"Yes."

"I don't cheat on my husband so if you gon' fuck me you gotta fuck him too."

"I'm down for whatever."

"When we get on the ship, I'll let you know when and where,"

"Okay, that's fine with me."

"Keep your mouth closed and don't let this get back to my boys. This is a one-time thing so keep that in mind, and when it's over, forget it ever happened."

"You got my word on that."

Faye winked at her and walked off with an extra twitch in her hips. Pop's had a surprise coming— right in the middle of the Atlantic ocean.

"Let me tell you niggas some real shit about how far a nigga will go for love, and how far a nigga will go when he feel like he found real love," Pops told Big Dre, and the rest of the boys. "Money and bitches are the number one cause in tearing down friendships."

Short Dogg was still asleep, or so they thought. But he was just relaxing with his eyes closed, thinking about all that had gone on over the past few weeks.

"After me and Faye decided we were through with hittin' licks and decided to get married, there was still one thing she had to do to close the last chapter of her life with Connie and Omars dad.

I never got the chance to meet him 'cause he was already gone by the time I met Faye. But, she didn't wanna marry me until she had dealt with the niggas who had killed their dad."

"I thought he died in a car wreck?" Junior asked.

He did die in a car wreck but it wasn't just a regular car wreck. See, some niggas was chasing him."

"Mama never told us that," Junior said.

"She don't like talkin' about the shit 'cause the niggas were trying to get at their dad behind her."

"No shit!" Glenn said.

"What happened, Pops?" Jay asked.

"The shit went down like this…

It was December 31st, and Faye was just gettin' off work at the hospital where she was a LVN. She had showered and dressed at work and was headed to her best friends' house for a New Year party.

She pulled up and parked. There were a few people standing outside smoking. When she got out of her car, a guy named Rome was sitting in his car with his homeboy, Tree, in the passenger seat. Rome called Faye over to the car.

"What's up, Rome? Hey Tree."

"When you gon' let a nigga take you out?" Rome asked.

"Never, nigga, why you keep askin' me the same thing and you know the answer ain't gonna ever change?"

"You still fuckin' with that lame ass nigga Kyle?"

"Nigga, you a lame and that's my baby daddy so you know I'm still fuckin' with him. Ain't you still fuckin' with my best friend, Porscha?"

"That's all we doin' is fuckin'. She know how I roll, and I aint tryna be tied down to no bitch."

"Yeah, we all know how you roll. Didn't Black Brenda give your dumb ass gonorrhea or something?" Faye said, walking off laughing.

"Okay, Faye, you got jokes, huh?"

Faye went inside and worked her way through the crowd and to the kitchen, where she found her best friend, Porscha, making drinks.

"What's up, girl?" she said, giving her a hug.

"Ain't shit, finna bring this New year in right. Kyle just called and said he was dropping the kids off at your Mama's house. Then he going to stop and see his brother before he come over here."

"Give me a glass of that Crown and let me go find me something to smoke."

"Sherry in the den rolling some blunts right now."

"Well, that's where I'm headed," Faye said, getting her cup and going to the den.

Kyle showed up right before the count down to the new year.

At 11:59 p.m., they turned the TV on and did the count down. "5-4-3-2-1- Happy New Year!" everyone shouted.

They made their new year's resolutions and then started dancing and celebrating.

"Happy New Year, baby," Kyle told her, as they danced to an old school slow jam.

"Happy New Year. What's your new year resolution? Two more kids."

"Bullshit. You must got you a side chick," she said laughing.

"Yeah, she due next month."

She stopped dancing and looked up at him and saw the smirk on his face. "Boy, stop playin' 'cause you was finna get your ass kicked."

"I don't want nobody but you."

As they were talking and dancing, Rome walked up and said, "Let me dance with her for a while."

"This one right here taken, my mans."

Quit cuffin', nigga, and let me dance with her fine ass."

"Rome, you drunk, so go on with that bullshit. I don't wanna dance with you."

"Bitch, you — " he started to say, before a two-piece from Kyle connected with his jaw and knocked him out.

"Hey, that's my homie," Tree said running up.

"Fuck your homie, nigga, and you too," Kyle said, before shooting a beautiful four-piece combination at him and then beat him silly.

"Y'all stop that shit... up in here fighting and we supposed to be celebrating," Porscha said.

"That's your dumb ass boyfriend," Faye said.

"I apologize Porscha but this nigga was way too disrespectful. We just gonna leave. Thank you for inviting us. We had fun," Kyle said. He grabbed Faye's hand and headed for the door.

"I'll call you tomorrow, girl," Porscha told Faye.

"Alright."

They left out of the door and went to their respective cars.

"I'll follow you," Faye said, getting in her car.

"Alright. I'ma stop at the gas station and fill up, my shit damn near on E."

"Your shit always on E," she said laughing.

They drove to the gas station down the street and Kyle gave her the money to pay for the gas. She went in and paid for the gas while he pumped it.

They left the gas station and stopped at a red light. Rome and Tree pulled up on the side of Kyle, and Tree leaned out the wimdow and started shooting. Kyle smashed the gas and drove off. He tried to make a turn at the next intersection but was going too fast and ran head first into the street light.

When Faye saw him hit the street light pole, she knew he wasn't wearing his seatbelt. Rome and Tree kept going.

She jumped out of her car and ran over to his car and looked in. She knew he was dead when she saw his head. She could see where his head hit the windshield and shattered the glass, which crushed his skull. She tried to get the door opened but she couldn't.

"You need some help?" an old White man asked.

"Yes, find a phone and call 9-1-1."

"There's a pay phone right down the street."

"Okay, thank you. Hurry, he's hurt bad," she said, holding back her tears.

She stayed until the ambulance and the police came. He was pronounced dead at the scene. It was New Years day and they blamed it on alcohol. She called his brother from the first pay phone she got to and told him that he had a wreck and was pronounced dead at the scene. She didn't even go to the hospital. She drove back to Porscha's house where she saw Rome's car parked outside. She sat in her car waiting and watching for one of them to come out.

About an hour later, Tree came out of the house and started walking toward his mother's house, who stayed about two blocks away.

Faye drove around the block and waited where she knew he would be coming. She got out and stood in the darkness, and when he walked up, she came out and shot him five times in the face and head. She calmly walked back to her car and drove away.

Three weeks later, Rome was sent to State jail for two years for an old, possession of a controlled substance, case. During his prison time, Faye met Pops.

A week after Rome got out, Faye sat down and told Pops the whole story about Kyle's death. She had never told anyone what happened that night. Faye told Pops that she couldn't marry him until she closed the final chapter of her life with Kyle, and that was to send Rome to his maker.

I'll get that nigga for you, just show me who the nigga is," Pops told her.

"Nah, I gotta do this."

From that day forward, they started watching Rome's mother's house until they saw him. They followed him for a week before they finally got the chance to get at him.

Rome had been hustling at the corner store all day and night trying to get back on his feet. One night about two in the morning, Rome was walking down the street to his mom's house where he'd been staying.

Faye stepped outta the dark and said, "This is for Kyle," and unloaded a whole clip in his chest.

When she got back in the car, tears were running down her face.

"You alright, baby?" Pops asked, holding her hand.

"Yeah, I'm good. We can get married now."

The Lane 2 Coming Soon.

Lock Down Publications and Ca$h Presents
Assisted Publishing Packages

BASIC PACKAGE $499 Editing Cover Design Formatting	**UPGRADED PACKAGE** $800 Typing Editing Cover Design Formatting
ADVANCE PACKAGE $1,200 Typing Editing Cover Design Formatting Copyright registration Proofreading Upload book to Amazon	**LDP SUPREME PACKAGE** $1,500 Typing Editing Cover Design Formatting Copyright registration Proofreading Set up Amazon account Upload book to Amazon Advertise on LDP, Amazon and Facebook Page

***Other services available upon request.
Additional charges may apply

Lock Down Publications
P.O. Box 944
Stockbridge, GA 30281-9998
Phone: 470 303-9761

Submission Guideline

Submit the first three chapters of your completed manuscript to ldpsubmissions@gmail.com. In the subject line add **Your Book's Title**. The manuscript must be in a Word Doc file and sent as an attachment. Document should be in Times New Roman, double spaced, and in size 12 font. Also, provide your synopsis and full contact information. If sending multiple submissions, they must each be in a separate email.

Have a story but no way to send it electronically? You can still submit to LDP/Ca$h Presents. Send in the first three chapters, written or typed, of your completed manuscript to:

LDP: Submissions Dept
P.O. Box 944
Stockbridge, GA 30281-9998

DO NOT send original manuscript. Must be a duplicate.
Provide your synopsis and a cover letter containing your full contact information.

Thanks for considering LDP and Ca$h Presents.

NEW RELEASES

SANCTIFIED AND HORNY
by **XTASY**

THE PLUG OF LIL MEXICO 2
by **CHRIS GREEN**

THE BLACK DIAMOND CARTEL
by **SAYNOMORE**

THE BIRTH OF A GANGSTER 3
by **DELMONT PLAYER**

Coming Soon from Lock Down Publications/Ca$h Presents

BLOOD OF A BOSS VI
SHADOWS OF THE GAME II
TRAP BASTARD II
By **Askari**

LOYAL TO THE GAME IV
By **T.J. & Jelissa**

TRUE SAVAGE VIII
MIDNIGHT CARTEL IV
DOPE BOY MAGIC IV
CITY OF KINGZ III
NIGHTMARE ON SILENT AVE II
THE PLUG OF LIL MEXICO II
CLASSIC CITY II
By **Chris Green**

BLAST FOR ME III
A SAVAGE DOPEBOY III
CUTTHROAT MAFIA III
DUFFLE BAG CARTEL VII
HEARTLESS GOON VI
By **Ghost**

A HUSTLER'S DECEIT III
KILL ZONE II
BAE BELONGS TO ME III
TIL DEATH II
By **Aryanna**

KING OF THE TRAP III
By **T.J. Edwards**

GORILLAZ IN THE BAY V
3X KRAZY III
STRAIGHT BEAST MODE III
By **De'Kari**

KINGPIN KILLAZ IV
STREET KINGS III
PAID IN BLOOD III
CARTEL KILLAZ IV
DOPE GODS III
By **Hood Rich**

SINS OF A HUSTLA II
By **ASAD**

YAYO V
BRED IN THE GAME 2
By **S. Allen**

THE STREETS WILL TALK II
By **Yolanda Moore**

SON OF A DOPE FIEND III
HEAVEN GOT A GHETTO III
SKI MASK MONEY III
By **Renta**

LOYALTY AIN'T PROMISED III
By **Keith Williams**

I'M NOTHING WITHOUT HIS LOVE II
SINS OF A THUG II
TO THE THUG I LOVED BEFORE II
IN A HUSTLER I TRUST II
By **Monet Dragun**

QUIET MONEY IV
EXTENDED CLIP III
THUG LIFE IV
By **Trai'Quan**

THE STREETS MADE ME IV
By **Larry D. Wright**

IF YOU CROSS ME ONCE III
ANGEL V
By **Anthony Fields**

THE STREETS WILL NEVER CLOSE IV
By **K'ajji**

HARD AND RUTHLESS III
KILLA KOUNTY IV
By **Khufu**

MONEY GAME III
By **Smoove Dolla**

MURDA WAS THE CASE III
Elijah R. Freeman

AN UNFORESEEN LOVE IV
BABY, I'M WINTERTIME COLD III
By **Meesha**

QUEEN OF THE ZOO III
By **Black Migo**

CONFESSIONS OF A JACKBOY III
By **Nicholas Lock**

JACK BOYS VS DOPE BOYS IV
A GANGSTA'S QUR'AN V
COKE GIRLZ II
COKE BOYS II
LIFE OF A SAVAGE V
CHI'RAQ GANGSTAS V
SOSA GANG III
BRONX SAVAGES II
BODYMORE KINGPINS II
By **Romell Tukes**

KING KILLA II
By **Vincent "Vitto" Holloway**

BETRAYAL OF A THUG III
By **Fre$h**

THE MURDER QUEENS III
By **Michael Gallon**

THE BIRTH OF A GANGSTER III
By **Delmont Player**

TREAL LOVE II
By **Le'Monica Jackson**

FOR THE LOVE OF BLOOD III
By **Jamel Mitchell**

RAN OFF ON DA PLUG II
By **Paper Boi Rari**

HOOD CONSIGLIERE III
By **Keese**

PRETTY GIRLS DO NASTY THINGS II
By **Nicole Goosby**

PROTÉGÉ OF A LEGEND III
LOVE IN THE TRENCHES II
By **Corey Robinson**

IT'S JUST ME AND YOU II
By **Ah'Million**

FOREVER GANGSTA III
By **Adrian Dulan**

GORILLAZ IN THE TRENCHES II
By **SayNoMore**

THE COCAINE PRINCESS VIII
By **King Rio**

CRIME BOSS II
By **Playa Ray**

LOYALTY IS EVERYTHING III
By **Molotti**

HERE TODAY GONE TOMORROW II
By **Fly Rock**

THE LANE | KEN-KEN SENCE

REAL G'S MOVE IN SILENCE II
By **Von Diesel**

GRIMEY WAYS IV
By **Ray Vinci**

Available Now

RESTRAINING ORDER I & II
By **CA$H & Coffee**

LOVE KNOWS NO BOUNDARIES I II & III
By **Coffee**

RAISED AS A GOON I, II, III & IV
BRED BY THE SLUMS I, II, III
BLAST FOR ME I & II
ROTTEN TO THE CORE I II III
A BRONX TALE I, II, III
DUFFLE BAG CARTEL I II III IV V VI
HEARTLESS GOON I II III IV V
A SAVAGE DOPEBOY I II
DRUG LORDS I II III
CUTTHROAT MAFIA I II
KING OF THE TRENCHES
By **Ghost**

LAY IT DOWN I & II
LAST OF A DYING BREED I II
BLOOD STAINS OF A SHOTTA I & II III
By **Jamaica**

LOYAL TO THE GAME I II III
LIFE OF SIN I, II III
By **TJ & Jelissa**

IF LOVING HIM IS WRONG…I & II
LOVE ME EVEN WHEN IT HURTS I II III
By **Jelissa**

THE LANE | KEN-KEN SENCE

BLOODY COMMAS I & II
SKI MASK CARTEL I, II & III
KING OF NEW YORK I II, III IV V
RISE TO POWER I II III
COKE KINGS I II III IV V
BORN HEARTLESS I II III IV
KING OF THE TRAP I II
By **T.J. Edwards**

WHEN THE STREETS CLAP BACK I & II III
THE HEART OF A SAVAGE I II III IV
MONEY MAFIA I II
LOYAL TO THE SOIL I II III
By **Jibril Williams**

A DISTINGUISHED THUG STOLE MY HEART I II &
III
LOVE SHOULDN'T HURT I II III IV
RENEGADE BOYS I II III IV
PAID IN KARMA I II III
SAVAGE STORMS I II III
AN UNFORESEEN LOVE I II III
BABY, I'M WINTERTIME COLD I II
By **Meesha**

A GANGSTER'S CODE I &, II III
A GANGSTER'S SYN I II III
THE SAVAGE LIFE I II III
CHAINED TO THE STREETS I II III
BLOOD ON THE MONEY I II III
A GANGSTA'S PAIN I II III
By **J-Blunt**

PUSH IT TO THE LIMIT
By **Bre' Hayes**

BLOOD OF A BOSS I, II, III, IV, V
SHADOWS OF THE GAME
TRAP BASTARD
By **Askari**

THE STREETS BLEED MURDER I, II & III
THE HEART OF A GANGSTA I II& III
By **Jerry Jackson**

CUM FOR ME I II III IV V VI VII VIII
An **LDP Erotica Collaboration**

BRIDE OF A HUSTLA I II & II
THE FETTI GIRLS I, II& III
CORRUPTED BY A GANGSTA I, II III, IV
BLINDED BY HIS LOVE
THE PRICE YOU PAY FOR LOVE I, II ,III
DOPE GIRL MAGIC I II III
By **Destiny Skai**

WHEN A GOOD GIRL GOES BAD
By **Adrienne**

A GANGSTER'S REVENGE I II III & IV
THE BOSS MAN'S DAUGHTERS I II III IV V
A SAVAGE LOVE I & II
BAE BELONGS TO ME I II
A HUSTLER'S DECEIT I, II, III
WHAT BAD BITCHES DO I, II, III
SOUL OF A MONSTER I II III
KILL ZONE
A DOPE BOY'S QUEEN I II III
TIL DEATH
By **Aryanna**

THE COST OF LOYALTY I II III
By Kweli

A KINGPIN'S AMBITION
A KINGPIN'S AMBITION **II**
I MURDER FOR THE DOUGH
By **Ambitious**

TRUE SAVAGE I II III IV V VI VII
DOPE BOY MAGIC I, II, III
MIDNIGHT CARTEL I II III
CITY OF KINGZ I II
NIGHTMARE ON SILENT AVE
THE PLUG OF LIL MEXICO II
CLASSIC CITY
By **Chris Green**

A DOPEBOY'S PRAYER
By **Eddie "Wolf" Lee**

THE KING CARTEL I, II & III
By **Frank Gresham**

THESE NIGGAS AIN'T LOYAL I, II & III
By **Nikki Tee**

GANGSTA SHYT I II &III
By **CATO**

THE ULTIMATE BETRAYAL
By **Phoenix**

BOSS'N UP I, II & III
By **Royal Nicole**

THE LANE | KEN-KEN SENCE

I LOVE YOU TO DEATH
By **Destiny J**

I RIDE FOR MY HITTA
I STILL RIDE FOR MY HITTA
By **Misty Holt**

LOVE & CHASIN' PAPER
By **Qay Crockett**

TO DIE IN VAIN
SINS OF A HUSTLA
By **ASAD**

BROOKLYN HUSTLAZ
By **Boogsy Morina**

BROOKLYN ON LOCK I & II
By **Sonovia**

GANGSTA CITY
By **Teddy Duke**

A DRUG KING AND HIS DIAMOND I & II III
A DOPEMAN'S RICHES
HER MAN, MINE'S TOO I, II
CASH MONEY HO'S
THE WIFEY I USED TO BE I II
PRETTY GIRLS DO NASTY THINGS
By Nicole Goosby

LIPSTICK KILLAH I, II, III
CRIME OF PASSION I II & III
FRIEND OR FOE I II III
By **Mimi**

TRAPHOUSE KING I II & III
KINGPIN KILLAZ I II III
STREET KINGS I II
PAID IN BLOOD I II
CARTEL KILLAZ I II III
DOPE GODS I II
By **Hood Rich**

STEADY MOBBN' I, II, III
THE STREETS STAINED MY SOUL I II III
By **Marcellus Allen**

WHO SHOT YA I, II, III
SON OF A DOPE FIEND I II
HEAVEN GOT A GHETTO I II
SKI MASK MONEY I II
By **Renta**

GORILLAZ IN THE BAY I II III IV
TEARS OF A GANGSTA I II
3X KRAZY I II
STRAIGHT BEAST MODE I II
By **DE'KARI**

TRIGGADALE I II III
MURDA WAS THE CASE I II
By **Elijah R. Freeman**

THE STREETS ARE CALLING
By **Duquie Wilson**

SLAUGHTER GANG I II III
RUTHLESS HEART I II III
By **Willie Slaughter**

THE LANE | KEN-KEN SENCE

GOD BLESS THE TRAPPERS I, II, III
THESE SCANDALOUS STREETS I, II, III
FEAR MY GANGSTA I, II, III IV, V
THESE STREETS DON'T LOVE NOBODY I, II
BURY ME A G I, II, III, IV, V
A GANGSTA'S EMPIRE I, II, III, IV
THE DOPEMAN'S BODYGAURD I II
THE REALEST KILLAZ I II III
THE LAST OF THE OGS I II III
By **Tranay Adams**

MARRIED TO A BOSS I II III
By **Destiny Skai & Chris Green**

KINGZ OF THE GAME I II III IV V VI VII
CRIME BOSS
By **Playa Ray**

FUK SHYT
By **Blakk Diamond**

DON'T F#CK WITH MY HEART I II
By **Linnea**

ADDICTED TO THE DRAMA I II III
IN THE ARM OF HIS BOSS II
By **Jamila**

YAYO I II III IV
A SHOOTER'S AMBITION I II
BRED IN THE GAME
By **S. Allen**

LOYALTY AIN'T PROMISED I II
By **Keith Williams**

THE LANE | KEN-KEN SENCE

TRAP GOD I II III
RICH $AVAGE I II III
MONEY IN THE GRAVE I II III
By **Martell Troublesome Bolden**

FOREVER GANGSTA I II
GLOCKS ON SATIN SHEETS I II
By **Adrian Dulan**

TOE TAGZ I II III IV
LEVELS TO THIS SHYT I II
IT'S JUST ME AND YOU
By **Ah'Million**

KINGPIN DREAMS I II III
RAN OFF ON DA PLUG
By **Paper Boi Rari**

CONFESSIONS OF A GANGSTA I II III IV
CONFESSIONS OF A JACKBOY I II
By **Nicholas Lock**

I'M NOTHING WITHOUT HIS LOVE
SINS OF A THUG
TO THE THUG I LOVED BEFORE
A GANGSTA SAVED XMAS
IN A HUSTLER I TRUST
By **Monet Dragun**

QUIET MONEY I II III
THUG LIFE I II III
EXTENDED CLIP I II
A GANGSTA'S PARADISE
By **Trai'Quan**

THE LANE | KEN-KEN SENCE

CAUGHT UP IN THE LIFE I II III
THE STREETS NEVER LET GO I II III
By **Robert Baptiste**

NEW TO THE GAME I II III
MONEY, MURDER & MEMORIES I II III
By **Malik D. Rice**

CREAM I II III
THE STREETS WILL TALK
By **Yolanda Moore**

LIFE OF A SAVAGE I II III IV
A GANGSTA'S QUR'AN I II III IV
MURDA SEASON I II III
GANGLAND CARTEL I II III
CHI'RAQ GANGSTAS I II III IV
KILLERS ON ELM STREET I II III
JACK BOYZ N DA BRONX I II III
A DOPEBOY'S DREAM I II III
JACK BOYS VS DOPE BOYS I II III
COKE GIRLZ
COKE BOYS
SOSA GANG I II
BRONX SAVAGES
BODYMORE KINGPINS
By **Romell Tukes**

THE STREETS MADE ME I II III
By **Larry D. Wright**

CONCRETE KILLA I II III
VICIOUS LOYALTY I II III
By **Kingpen**

THE LANE | KEN-KEN SENCE

THE ULTIMATE SACRIFICE I, II, III, IV, V, VI
KHADIFI
IF YOU CROSS ME ONCE I II
ANGEL I II III IV
IN THE BLINK OF AN EYE
By **Anthony Fields**

THE LIFE OF A HOOD STAR
By **Ca$h & Rashia Wilson**

THE STREETS WILL NEVER CLOSE I II III
By **K'ajji**

NIGHTMARES OF A HUSTLA I II III
By **King Dream**

HARD AND RUTHLESS I II
MOB TOWN 251
THE BILLIONAIRE BENTLEYS I II III
REAL G'S MOVE IN SILENCE
By **Von Diesel**

GHOST MOB
By **Stilloan Robinson**

MOB TIES I II III IV V VI
SOUL OF A HUSTLER, HEART OF A KILLER I II
GORILLAZ IN THE TRENCHES
By **SayNoMore**

BODYMORE MURDERLAND I II III
THE BIRTH OF A GANGSTER I II
By **Delmont Player**

THE LANE | KEN-KEN SENCE

FOR THE LOVE OF A BOSS
By **C. D. Blue**

KILLA KOUNTY I II III IV
By Khufu

MOBBED UP I II III IV
THE BRICK MAN I II III IV V
THE COCAINE PRINCESS I II III IV V VI VII
By **King Rio**

MONEY GAME I II
By **Smoove Dolla**

A GANGSTA'S KARMA I II III
By **FLAME**

KING OF THE TRENCHES I II III
By **GHOST & TRANAY ADAMS**

QUEEN OF THE ZOO I II
By **Black Migo**

GRIMEY WAYS I II III
By **Ray Vinci**

XMAS WITH AN ATL SHOOTER
By **Ca$h & Destiny Skai**

KING KILLA
By **Vincent "Vitto" Holloway**

BETRAYAL OF A THUG I II
By **Fre$h**

THE LANE | KEN-KEN SENCE

THE MURDER QUEENS I II
By **Michael Gallon**

TREAL LOVE
By **Le'Monica Jackson**

FOR THE LOVE OF BLOOD I II
By **Jamel Mitchell**

HOOD CONSIGLIERE I II
By **Keese**

PROTÉGÉ OF A LEGEND I II
LOVE IN THE TRENCHES
By **Corey Robinson**

BORN IN THE GRAVE I II III
By **Self Made Tay**

MOAN IN MY MOUTH
By **XTASY**

TORN BETWEEN A GANGSTER AND A
GENTLEMAN
By **J-BLUNT & Miss Kim**

LOYALTY IS EVERYTHING I II
By **Molotti**

HERE TODAY GONE TOMORROW
By **Fly Rock**

PILLOW PRINCESS
By **S. Hawkins**

BOOKS BY LDP'S CEO, CA$H

TRUST IN NO MAN
TRUST IN NO MAN 2
TRUST IN NO MAN 3
BONDED BY BLOOD
SHORTY GOT A THUG
THUGS CRY
THUGS CRY 2
THUGS CRY 3
TRUST NO BITCH
TRUST NO BITCH 2
TRUST NO BITCH 3
TIL MY CASKET DROPS
RESTRAINING ORDER
RESTRAINING ORDER 2
IN LOVE WITH A CONVICT
LIFE OF A HOOD STAR
XMAS WITH AN ATL SHOOTER